'If I lived somewhere like this I would never want to leave,' she breathed wonderingly.

'If you lived here, neither would I,' Brice answered huskily from just behind her. Far too close behind her, Sabina discovered as she swung round, finding herself almost pressed against his chest, becoming very still, her breathing shallow.

It was as if time was standing still as they looked at each other in the twilight, Brice's face vividly clear to her, his eyes a sparkling emerald-green, the intimacy of his words lying heavily between them.

She should stop this, break the spell— except that was exactly what it felt like, as if she were bewitched, by both Brice and her surroundings...

She didn't move, couldn't move, clasping her hands together in front of her to stop them shaking. What was happening to her?

BACHELOR COUSINS

Three cousins of Scottish descent...
they're male, millionaires and they're marriageable!

Meet Logan, Fergus and Brice, three tall, dark, handsome men about town. They've made their millions in London, but their hearts belong to the heather-clad hills of their Grandfather McDonald's Scottish estate.

Logan, Fergus and Brice are all very intriguing characters. Logan likes his life exactly as it is, and is determined not to change—even for a woman...until scatty, emotional Darcy turns his neatly ordered world upside down! Fergus is clever, witty, laid-back and determined to view things in his own particular way...until the adorably petite Chloe begs him to change his mind—she's willing to pay any price to get him to agree! Finally, there's Brice: tough, resolute and determined, he's accountable to no one...until blue-eyed beauty Sabina makes him think again!

Logan, Fergus and Brice are about to give up their keenly fought-for bachelor status for three wonderful women—laugh, cry and read all about their trials and tribulations in their pursuit of love.

TO MARRY McALLISTER

BY
CAROLE MORTIMER

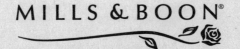

First published in Great Britain 2002
Harlequin Mills & Boon Limited,
Eton House, 18-24 Paradise Road, Richmond, Surrey TW9 1SR

© Carole Mortimer 2002

ISBN 0 263 82963 4

Set in Times Roman 10½ on 11¼ pt.
01-0902-49356

Printed and bound in Spain
by Litografía Rosés, S.A., Barcelona

CHAPTER ONE

'MCALLISTER, isn't it?'

Brice tensed resentfully at this intrusion into his solitude. If one could be solitary in the midst of a party to celebrate a political victory!

Ordinary he wouldn't have been at this party, but the youngest daughter of the newest Member of Parliament had married his cousin, Fergus, six months ago, and so all the family had been invited to Paul Hamilton's house today to join in the celebrations at his re-election. It would have seemed churlish for Brice to have refused.

But he didn't particularly care for being addressed by just his surname—it reminded him all too forcefully of his schooldays. Although it was the man's tone of voice that irritated him the most: arrogance bordering on condescension!

He turned slowly, finding himself face to face with a man he knew he had never met before. Tall, blond hair silvered at the temples, probably aged in his mid-fifties, the hard handsomeness of the man's face was totally in keeping with that arrogance Brice had already guessed at.

'Brice McAllister, yes,' he corrected the other man coolly.

'Richard Latham.' The other man thrust out his hand in greeting.

Richard Latham... Somehow Brice knew he recognised the name, if not the man...

He shook the other man's hand briefly, deliberately not continuing the conversation. Never the most sociable of men, Brice considered he had done his bit today towards

family relations, was only waiting for a lull in the pro-
ceedings so that he could take his leave.

'You have absolutely no idea who I am, do you?' The
other man sounded amused at the idea rather than irritated.

Brice may not know *who* the other man was, but he did
know *what* he was—the persistent type!

Latham, he had said his name was. The same surname
as Paul Hamilton's other son-in-law, his own cousin
Fergus's brother-in-law, which meant he was probably
some sort of relative of the Hamilton family. But somehow
Brice had a feeling that wasn't what the other man meant.

He held back his sigh of impatience. It was almost seven
o'clock now; he had been looking forward to being able
to excuse himself shortly, on the pretext of having another
appointment this evening. But now he would have to ex-
tricate himself from this unwanted conversation first.

'I'm afraid not,' he returned without apology; being ac-
costed at a social gathering by a complete stranger wasn't
altogether unknown to him, but it certainly wasn't something he enjoyed.

Although, he accepted, being an artist of some repute,
that he had to show a certain social face. This man, with
his unmistakable arrogance, just seemed to have set his
teeth on edge from the start.

Richard Latham raised blond brows at the bluntness of
the admission. 'My secretary has contacted you twice during the last month, concerning a portrait of my fiancée I
would like to commission from you.'

He was *that* Richard Latham! Multimillionaire, jet-
setting businessman, the other man's business interests
ranging worldwide, his personal relationships with some
of the world's most beautiful women making newspaper
headlines almost as much as his successful business ven-
tures. Although Brice had no idea who the 'fiancée' he had
just mentioned could be.

He shook his head. 'As I explained in my letter, in reply

to your secretary's first enquiry, I'm afraid I don't do portraits,' he drawled politely. And he hadn't felt the least inclination to explain that all over again in reply to the second letter he had received from this man's secretary only a week later.

'Not true,' Richard Latham came back abruptly, blue eyes narrowed assessingly on Brice's deliberately impassive expression. 'I've seen the rather magnificent one you did of Darcy McKenzie.'

Brice smiled slightly. 'Darcy happens to be my cousin-in-law. She is married to my cousin Logan.'

'And?' Richard Latham rasped frowningly.

Brice shrugged. 'It was a one-off. A wedding gift.'

The other man gave an arrogant inclination of his head. 'This is a gift too—to myself.'

And he was obviously a man, Brice acknowledged ruefully, who wasn't used to hearing the word no—from anyone!

Well, Brice couldn't help that, he simply did not paint portraits, had no inclination to paint a flattering likeness of the rich and the pampered, just so that they could hang it on one of the walls of their elegant homes and claim it was a 'McAllister'.

'I really am sorry—' he began—only to come to an abrupt halt as the room suddenly fell silent, all attention on the woman who now stood in the doorway.

Sabina.

Brice had seen photographs the last few years of the world's most famous model—he would have to have been blind not to have done. Hardly a day passed when she wasn't photographed appearing in some fashion show or other, at a party, or public event. But none of those photographs had prepared Brice for the sheer perfection of her beauty, the creaminess of her skin against the short, shimmering silver dress she wore, her legs extremely long and shapely, her eyes a luminous blue, long hair the colour of ripe wheat reaching almost to her slender waist.

She wore absolutely no jewellery, but then she didn't need to; it would merely be gilding the lily.

His attention returned to her eyes. Luminous, yes, with a black ring encircling the sky-blue of the iris. But there was something else there he picked up on as she looked about the room. A certain apprehension. Almost fear…?

Then a shutter came down over those amazing blue eyes, the emotion masked almost as quickly as Brice's trained eye had recognised it, her smile confident now as she looked across the room in his direction.

'Excuse me while I greet my fiancée,' Richard Latham murmured mockingly before leaving Brice's side to stride forcefully across the room to kiss Sabina warmly on the cheek, his arm moving possessively about her slender shoulders even as she smiled at him.

Brice realised as he watched the two of them that he had been wrong about the jewellery; on the third finger of Sabina's left hand gleamed a huge heart-shaped diamond.

Sabina was the fiancée Richard Latham had referred to? The fiancée he wanted Brice to paint a portrait of…?

The one woman in the world, now that he had seen her in the flesh, that Brice knew he simply had to paint!

Oh, not because of her beauty, spectacular though it might be. No, it was that quickly masked emotion that intrigued Brice, that momentary glimpse of fear and vulnerability, that made Sabina more than just a beautiful woman.

It was an emotion he wanted to explore, if only on canvas…

'Sorry I'm a little late.' Sabina smiled warmly at Richard. 'I'm afraid Andrew was being extremely difficult over fittings today.' She grimaced as she lightly dismissed one of the top fashion designers of the day. Andrew might be at the top, but he had a volatile temper to go with it, which made him hell to work for.

'You're here now, that's all that matters,' Richard assured her lightly as he turned back into the room.

Sabina's tension left her. How nice it was to have someone in her life who was never difficult over the demands of her career. In fact, it was the opposite where Richard was concerned; her famous face as she stood at his side was all that he wanted from her.

And, thankfully, the conversation seemed to have resumed in the room again now. Even after seven years as a top model, Sabina didn't think she would ever get used to the way people stopped to stare at her wherever she went, had had to build up a veneer over the years to cover up the dismay she often felt at the effect her looks had on people.

The only place she seemed to get away from being recognised was when she went to one of her favourite hamburger restaurants. No one ever believed, with her willowy slenderness, that it could possibly be the model Sabina, dressed in denims and casual top, her hair hidden under a baseball cap, sitting there eating a hamburger with French fries! But, sceptical as some reporters were, claiming she lived on lettuce leaves and water to maintain her slender figure, she was actually one of those lucky people who could eat anything and never put on weight.

Although, she acknowledged a little sadly, she hadn't dared to make one of those impromptu visits to eat one of her favourite foods for some time now. Six months, in fact...

'I have someone I want you to meet, Sabina,' Richard told her smoothly now. 'And someone I want to meet you,' he added with a certain amount of satisfaction.

Sabina looked at him enquiringly, but could read nothing from his expression as he guided her across the room to meet the man she had seen him talking to when she'd arrived.

The other man was tall, even taller than Richard's six feet two inches, probably aged in his mid-thirties, dressed casually in blue denims teamed with a white tee shirt and black jacket, with over-long dark hair, and a face of austere handsomeness. But it was the green eyes in that face that caught and held Sabina's attention, eyes of such perception they seemed to see right into the soul.

Sabina felt the return of her earlier apprehension run down the length of her spine; she didn't want anyone, least of all this austere stranger, looking into her soul!

'Brice, I would like you to meet my fiancée, Sabina. Sabina, this is Brice McAllister,' Richard introduced lightly.

But again, unless Sabina was mistaken, Richard's voice contained that element of satisfaction as he made the introductions.

She knew Richard was proud of the way she looked, but at this moment he seemed more so than usual.

She looked curiously at the other man. Brice McAllister. Should she know—? The artist! Brice McAllister, she knew, was one of the most sought-after artists in the world today. But that still didn't explain Richard's attitude towards the other man...

'Mr McAllister,' she greeted coolly.

'Sabina.' He nodded abruptly. 'Do you have a surname?' he added mockingly.

'Smith,' she supplied dryly. 'But not many people know that. My mother's more exotic choice of a first name was an effort to make up for the lack of imagination in my surname.' And she, Sabina realised with a frown, was talking merely for the sake of it. And to a man who instinctively made her uneasy.

But she couldn't seem to help it when those deep green eyes were looking at her so intently...

'You're Sabina. It's enough,' Richard put in with a certain amount of arrogance.

Did Richard sense it too, that deep intensity coming from that unblinking, emerald-green gaze?

Sabina felt that shiver once again down the length of her spine, moving slightly closer to Richard as she did so.

'I promise not to tell a soul,' Brice McAllister drawled playfully in answer to her earlier remark.

Although somehow it didn't sound playful coming from this man. Neither was the mention of the 'soul' to Sabina—when she was sure this man could see straight into hers!

What would he see? she wondered. Warmth and kindness, she hoped. Humour and laughter, too. Loyalty and honour. Apprehension and fear—

No! She was careful to keep those emotions under lock and key. Although that wasn't so easy to achieve when she was alone. Which was why she very rarely allowed herself to be alone with her thoughts any more...

'Your fiancée and I were just discussing the possibility of my painting your portrait,' Brice McAllister bit out evenly.

Sabina gave a perplexed frown as she turned to look at Richard. He hadn't mentioned anything about having her portrait painted. And she already knew, from the little time she had spent in Brice McAllister's brooding company, that he was the last man she wanted to spend time with!

'I'm afraid Brice has just ruined my surprise.' Richard laughed dismissively, giving her shoulders a warm squeeze before turning to look challengingly at the younger man. 'You've decided you would like to paint Sabina's portrait after all?' he drawled mockingly.

Sabina looked at Brice McAllister, too, gathering from Richard's comment that the question of painting her portrait hadn't been as cut and dried as the artist had just implied it was...

If not, why had he changed his mind?

If he had…

Brice McAllister shrugged unconcernedly. 'It's a possibility,' he replied noncommittally. 'I would need to do a few preliminary sketches before making any definite decision.' He grimaced. 'But I should warn you now, I don't do chocolate-box likenesses of people.'

The implication being that she had a chocolate-box beauty! Not exactly the most charming man she had ever met, Sabina acknowledged ruefully, although he was at least honest.

But maybe that was what he meant about not doing 'chocolate-box' likenesses of people, Sabina realised with a faint stirring of unease; he liked to capture what was inside the person as well as a physical likeness. Maybe her instinct had been right after all and he really could see into her soul…?

'A "warts and all" man,' Richard realised dryly. 'Well, as you can clearly see, Sabina doesn't have a single blemish.' He looked at her proudly.

Sabina looked at Brice McAllister, only to look quickly away again as she saw the open derision in his expression at Richard's obviously possessive praise. But the intensity of the artist's attention on her didn't seem to allow him to see Richard's possession for exactly what it was: simply pride in ownership of an object of beauty.

'I think you could be slightly biased, Richard,' she told him huskily. 'And I'm sure we must have taken up enough of Mr McAllister's time for one evening…' she added pointedly, wanting to get away from the intensity of that probing green gaze.

She didn't like Brice McAllister, she decided. Something about the way he looked at her made her feel uncomfortable. And the sooner she and Richard distanced themselves from him, the better she would like it.

'If I could just have your address and telephone number…' Brice McAllister drawled questioningly. 'Perhaps I can ring you, and we can sort out a time convenient to both of us for those sketches?'

Sabina swallowed hard, very reluctant for Brice McAllister to know any more about her than he already did.

'That's easy, they're the same as mine,' Richard informed Brice mockingly even as he took one of his personal cards from his wallet and handed it to the other man. 'If neither Sabina nor I are at home when you call, my housekeeper can always take a message,' he added lightly.

Sabina could feel the increased intensity of that dark green gaze now as Brice McAllister digested the knowledge of her living at Richard's Mayfair home with him. His mouth had thinned disapprovingly, those green eyes cool as his gaze raked over her assessingly.

Sabina challengingly withstood the derision now obvious in Brice McAllister's expression as he looked at her, although she had no control over the heated colour that had entered her cheeks.

Damn him, who did he think he was to stand there and make judgements about her behaviour? She was twenty-five years old, for goodness' sake, quite old enough to make her own choices and decisions. Without being answerable to anyone but herself. And she was quite happy with her living arrangements, thank you!

If a little defensive…?

Maybe. But Brice McAllister didn't know of the understanding she and Richard had come to when they'd become engaged several months ago, could have no idea that engagement was only a front, that their engagement was based on liking, not love. A protective shield for her from the fear she had lived with the last six months, in exchange for that object of beauty—herself!—that Richard wanted so badly in his life. And, strangely enough, she had realised over the last few months, that was all he wanted from her...

No doubt to a third person their arrangement would seem odd in the extreme, but it suited them. And it was certainly none of this man's business!

'I'll call you,' Brice McAllister drawled derisively, putting Richard's card in the breast pocket of his jacket before giving a dismissive nod of his head. Leaving them, he strolled over to join a couple sitting in the corner of the room cooing over a very young baby.

'Brice's cousin, Logan McKenzie, and his lovely wife Darcy,' Richard murmured softly at her side.

Sabina didn't care who the other couple were, or what relationship they had to the arrogant Brice McAllister; she was just glad to have him gone. She could breathe easily again now!

In truth, she hadn't even realised she had been holding her breath until he'd left them, and then she had been forced to take in a huge gulp of air—or expire!

One thing she did know—she had no intention of being at home if Brice McAllister should choose to telephone her.

And, in the meantime, she intended doing everything she could to persuade Richard into changing his mind about wanting Brice McAllister to paint her...

CHAPTER TWO

'BUT I'm afraid Miss Sabina isn't at home,' Richard Latham's housekeeper informed him for what had to be the half-dozenth time in a week.

Actually, Brice knew exactly how many times he had telephoned and been informed 'Miss Sabina isn't at home'. It was the fifth time, and his temper was verging on breaking-point. Mainly, he knew, because he was sure he was being given the run-around by the beautiful Sabina.

He had known by the expression on her face at Paul Hamilton's house the previous week, when told that Richard wanted Brice to paint her portrait, that Sabina didn't share that desire.

Which, if he were honest, only made Brice all the more determined to do it.

'Thanks for your help,' Brice answered the housekeeper distractedly, wondering where he went from here. Telephoning to make an appointment to sketch Sabina obviously wasn't working!

'I'll tell Miss Sabina you rang,' the woman informed him before ringing off.

A lot of good that would do him, Brice acknowledged impatiently as he replaced his own receiver. She had probably been informed of those other four calls he had made too—and, despite the fact that he had left his own telephone number, Sabina hadn't returned any of them.

'I would stay away from my Uncle Richard, if I were you,' David Latham had informed him ruefully at the party last week once the other man and Sabina had left. 'He's a collector of priceless items—and he considers Sabina part of that collection. He also brings a whole new meaning to the phrase ''black-sheep of the family'',' David had added with a grimace.

Richard Latham wasn't the one Brice was interested in. Although, as he was quickly learning, there seemed to be no other avenue to reach the beautiful Sabina...

For such an obviously public figure, she was actually quite reclusive, was never seen anywhere without the attentive Richard, or one of his employees, at her side.

Brice knew, because he had even attended a charity fashion show the previous weekend with his cousin Fergus, and his designer wife, Chloe, at which he'd known Sabina had been making an appearance. Only to have come up against the brick wall of what had appeared to be a bodyguard when he'd tried to go backstage after the show to talk to Sabina.

She hadn't joined the champagne reception after the show either, and discreet enquiries had told Brice that Sabina had been whisked away in a private car immediately after her turn on the catwalk had been over.

Sabina brought a whole new meaning to the word elusive—and, quite frankly, Brice had had enough.

He was also pretty sure that Richard Latham would have no idea Sabina had been avoiding his calls; the other man had been so determined to have Brice paint Sabina.

It wasn't too far to drive to Richard Latham's Mayfair home, the single car in the driveway, a sporty Mercedes, telling him that someone was at home. At this particular moment it didn't matter whether it was Richard Latham or Sabina—he intended getting that promised appointment from one of them!

He didn't know why, but he had been slightly surprised the previous week when Richard Latham had informed him that he and Sabina shared a home—and presumably a bed? There was something untouchable about Sabina, an aloofness that held her apart from everyone around her. Obviously that didn't include Richard Latham!

'Yes?'

Brice had been so lost in thought that he hadn't been aware of the door being opened to his ring on the bell, the elderly woman now looking up at him enquiringly obviously the housekeeper he had spoken to on the telephone over the last week.

'I would like to see Sabina,' Brice stated determinedly.

The woman raised dark brows. 'Do you have an appointment?'

If he did, then he would have no reason to be here!

Brice bit back his anger with effort. After all, it wasn't this woman he was angry with. 'Could you just tell Sabina that Mr McAllister would like to see her?' he rasped curtly.

'McAllister?' the woman repeated with a frown, giving a backward glance into the hallway behind her. 'But aren't you—?'

'The man who has telephoned half a dozen times this last week to speak to Sabina? Yes, I am,' Brice confirmed impatiently. 'Now could you please tell Sabina that I'm here?' He knew he wasn't being very polite, that it wasn't this woman's fault Sabina was giving him the brush-off, but at the moment he was just in too foul a mood to be fobbed off any longer.

Because he was utterly convinced, after that slightly furtive glance back into the house by the housekeeper, that the sporty Mercedes in the driveway belonged to Sabina, that she had been at home earlier when he'd telephoned, as she was at home now. She was just choosing not to take his calls.

'But—'

'It's all right, Mrs Clark,' Sabina assured smoothly as the door opened wider and she suddenly appeared beside the housekeeper in the doorway. 'Would you like to come through to the sitting-room, Mr McAllister?' she invited coolly.

He nodded abruptly, afraid to speak for the moment—

he might just say something he would later regret. Strange, he had never thought he had much of a temper, but this last week of having Sabina avoid him had certainly tried his patience.

She looked different again today, was wearing faded denims and a white cropped tee shirt, her long hair secured in a single braid down her spine, her face appearing bare of make-up. Brice had no idea how old she was, but at the moment she looked about eighteen!

'You'll have to excuse me, I'm afraid.' She indicated her casual appearance with a grimace as she turned to face him once the two of them were alone in the sitting-room. 'I've just got back from the gym.'

Brice raised dark, sceptical brows. 'Just?'

She met his gaze unflinchingly. 'Can I offer you some tea?'

'No, thanks,' he refused dryly. 'I've telephoned you several times this last week,' he added hardly.

Her gaze shifted slightly, no longer quite meeting his. 'Have you?' she returned uninterestedly.

Damn it, this really shouldn't be this difficult. Richard Latham was the one who had come to him with this commission—Brice hadn't even wanted to do it.

Until he'd seen Sabina...

'You know damn well I have,' he snapped impatiently.

She shrugged. 'I've been so busy this week. A trip to Paris. Several shows here. A photographic session with—'

'I'm not interested in what you've been doing, Sabina— only in why you've been avoiding my calls,' he rasped harshly.

'I've just told you—'

'Nothing,' he bit out tersely. 'Even if you haven't been here—' of which he was highly sceptical '—I'm sure the efficient Mrs Clark has informed you of each and every one of my telephone calls.'

'Perhaps,' Sabina conceded noncommittally. 'Are you sure I can't offer you any tea?'

'I'm absolutely positive,' he bit out between clenched teeth. A neat whisky would go down very well at the moment, but as it was only four o'clock in the afternoon he would give that a miss too for the moment. But the coolness of this woman was enough to drive any man to drink! 'Now, about that appointment—'

'Please, do sit down,' she invited lightly.

'Thanks—I would rather stand,' he grated harshly, this woman's aloofness doing nothing to alleviate his temper.

Sabina shrugged off his refusal before sitting down in one of the armchairs. 'Strange, but I was under the impression you were an artist of some repute?' she murmured dryly.

Brice eyed her guardedly. 'I am.'

'Really?' she mused derisively. 'And do you usually go chasing after commissions in this way?'

She was meaning to be insulting—and she was succeeding, Brice feeling the tide of anger that swept over him.

But at the same time he questioned why she was trying to antagonise him into refusing to paint her portrait before walking out of here. Because he knew that was exactly what she was trying to do.

He drew in a deeply controlling breath. 'Perhaps I will have that cup of tea, after all,' he drawled, before making himself comfortable in the armchair opposite hers.

But his gaze didn't leave the cool beauty of her face, meaning he missed none of the dismay at his words that she wasn't quick enough to mask. And Brice knew, despite having invited him to have tea in the first place, that Sabina actually wanted him out of here as quickly as possible.

Because Richard Latham might return at any moment and put paid to any effort on her part to elude having Brice paint her portrait…?

'I'm not in any hurry.' He made himself more comfortable in the armchair.

'Fine,' Sabina bit out in clipped tones, standing up gracefully. 'I'll just go and speak to Mrs Clark.'

And also take time to compose herself, Brice easily guessed. He knew he wasn't mistaken now, was absolutely sure that Sabina had no intention of letting him paint her portrait.

Why? What was it about him that she didn't like? Although Brice was sure it wasn't actually dislike he had seen in her eyes in that brief unguarded moment. It had been something approaching the fear he had sensed when he'd first seen her a week ago...

Sabina didn't go straight to the kitchen, running up the stairs to her bedroom first to splash cold water on her heated cheeks.

It had never occurred to her, when she'd refused to take any of Brice's telephone calls this last week, that he would actually come here!

But now she realised that perhaps it should have done; there was a ruthless determination about Brice McAllister that clearly stated he did not like to be thwarted. And never being available for his calls would definitely fall into that category in his eyes. Sabina now realised her mistake, knew that she should have taken one of his calls, if only to put him off coming here in person.

Well, it was too late now. Richard should be back within the hour, which meant she would have to hurry Brice McAllister through his tea, put up all sorts of obstacles to any immediate appointment to go to his studio, and then continue to cancel them thereafter.

Because she was even more convinced by this second meeting with him that she did not want Brice McAllister to paint her. She knew that he was every bit as good an artist as he had been proclaimed, and she also knew the reason that he was so good; Brice McAllister was exactly what she had thought him to be last week. He was a soul-searcher.

Those green eyes saw beyond the layers of social façade, past the protective barriers, straight into the soul, and deep into the real emotions that made a person exactly what they were, and what had made them that way. What had changed her from being happily sociable into a woman who now put up a protective barrier she was determined no one would penetrate?

'Tea will be through in a moment,' she announced lightly a few minutes later when she rejoined him in the sitting-room. 'Richard tells me that you have painted a rather magnificent portrait of your cousin's wife, Darcy McKenzie?' she prompted politely as she sat down.

He nodded abruptly. 'So I've been told.'

Sabina gave a bright, meaningless smile. 'I think he's hoping you will do as magnificent a one of me.'

Brice McAllister looked across at her with narrowed eyes. 'And what do you hope, Sabina?' he drawled.

He didn't really need to ask her that. Sabina was sure he already knew exactly what she hoped—that he wouldn't paint her at all, that he would just go away, and leave her with her barrier intact...

'The same thing, of course,' she returned smoothly, meeting that continuous probing gaze with a completely blank one of her own.

'Of course,' Brice finally echoed dryly. 'I—'

'Ah, tea.' Sabina turned to smile at Mrs Clark as she came into the room, the tray she carried, as Sabina had instructed the housekeeper a few minutes ago, containing just the tea; she did not intend offering Brice McAllister cake as well and delaying his departure by even a few minutes!

'No sugar for me, thanks,' Brice McAllister murmured

as the housekeeper left the room and Sabina sat forward to pour milk and tea into the cups.

'Sweet enough already' didn't quite apply to this man, Sabina acknowledged wryly. Tough, determined, slightly arrogant, very insightful, but Brice McAllister was definitely not 'sweet'!

'You seem quite at home here,' he drawled mockingly.

Despite being caught slightly off guard by the abruptness of the statement, Sabina managed to continue to calmly pour her own tea into the cup. 'Why shouldn't I? It is my home,' she returned coolly, once again sensing that disapproval of the fact that she lived here with Richard.

Which was slightly old-fashioned coming from a man who was probably only aged in his mid-thirties. Or perhaps it was the age difference between herself and Richard that Brice McAllister disapproved of…?

'So when are you free to sit for some sketches for me?' he prompted suddenly.

She shook her head regretfully as she sat back to drink her tea. 'I have a very busy schedule for the next few months—'

'I'm sure you must have an hour free somewhere,' he challenged, his mouth twisted derisively.

An hour, yes, possibly even the odd day here and there. But she didn't wish to give any of that time to Brice McAllister.

'Possibly,' she dismissed. 'But even I deserve some time off for rest and relaxation.'

'Sitting in a chair while I sketch you is not exactly going to tire you,' he returned dryly.

No—but trying to keep that blank wall in her eyes for an hour or so, shutting his probing gaze out of her inner self, definitely would!

She shrugged. 'I'm afraid I don't have my diary available at the moment, but as soon as I do I'll check it over and give you a call,' she added dismissively, having noted that his teacup was now empty.

He raised dark brows, making no effort to stand up in preparation of leaving. 'Tomorrow is Saturday—surely you aren't busy all over the weekend too?'

Sabina held in her frustrated anger with effort. This man wasn't just determined, he was dogged!

He was also, she was slowly coming to realise, all the more intent on doing those sketches because he sensed her own reluctance not to have him do them.

She shook her head with feigned regret. 'I'm afraid Richard and I are away this weekend,' she was able to tell him with complete honesty. And some satisfaction, she admitted inwardly.

At least, she was allowed to feel that way for a few very brief moments—because she then became aware of the sound of Richard's car outside in the driveway!

Usually she was more than pleased to see him, feeling safer when he was around, but today her heart sank at the realisation that he was home. Because Richard, she knew, despite gentle hints from her this last week that she really didn't want her portrait painted, was very determined that it would be done. And he was equally determined that the artist of that portrait would be Brice McAllister.

'Pity,' Brice drawled, obviously not in the least convinced by her excuse.

He also wasn't yet aware that Richard had arrived home, and Sabina schooled her features into one of cool politeness so that Brice McAllister shouldn't see how dismayed she felt at having the two men meet again. Something she had desperately been trying to avoid!

Brice sighed. 'I wonder—'

'Sabina? Are you—?' Richard had come straight into the sitting-room on entering the house, coming to an abrupt halt as he saw Sabina wasn't alone, his gaze narrowing as he took in Brice McAllister's presence in the room, the used cups on the low table clearly stating that he had been here for some time.

'Richard!' Sabina stood up immediately to cross the room to her fiancé's side, linking her arm warmly with his as she smiled at him. 'Mr McAllister called round for tea,' she dismissed with a lightness she was far from feeling.

Brice hadn't exactly 'called around for tea', that had been merely incidental; he had really come here in order to corner her into making a definite appointment for those sketches!

Sabina looked across at him now, wondering exactly what he was going to say to Richard about his reason for being here.

Would he tell Richard of his five unacknowledged telephone calls this past week? Yes, she did know exactly how many times he had telephoned, had instructed the loyal Mrs Clark to repeatedly tell him she wasn't at home!

Would he now tell Richard of her evasive tactics?

She gave an inward groan just at the thought of it, having no doubts that Richard would not be pleased that she had deliberately been avoiding Brice McAllister this last week. Richard would also, once they were alone, want to know the reason for it. She could hardly tell him that she had done it because she didn't want Brice McAllister looking into her soul…!

'I called round in person to apologise for not getting in touch with either of you this last week.' Brice McAllister was speaking smoothly now. 'I've been rather busy, I'm afraid. But that's still no excuse for my tardiness.' He grimaced.

Sabina could only stare across at him disbelievingly. He had been rather busy…? His tardiness…? He was the one apologising…? When she had been the one who—

'That's quite all right,' Richard accepted lightly, the tension relaxing from his body at the other man's explanation.

'Is everything sorted out now?' He looked at the two of them enquiringly.

Sabina looked at Brice for guidance on this one, still stunned by the way he had smoothed over the situation with a few brief—if totally inaccurate—words.

Had they sorted everything out now?

More to the point, why had Brice McAllister lied just now? Only she could benefit from such a misconception—and, as she was only too well aware, she had done nothing in their acquaintance so far to merit such gallantry. As Brice, up to that point, had done nothing to show he was capable of such an emotion!

He looked at her enquiringly. 'I believe so,' he drawled pointedly.

That was why he had lied—so that she had no choice but to make a firm appointment to go and see him. But, in the circumstances, it was probably the least that she owed him...

'Richard, I was just explaining to Mr McAllister—'

'Brice,' he put in dryly.

'To Brice,' she corrected after a slightly irritated glance in his direction; she did not want to be on a first-name basis with this man, intended keeping him very firmly at arm's length. Further, if she could manage it! 'That I have the afternoon free on Tuesday,' she admitted reluctantly.

'And I was just complimenting Sabina on having such a good memory,' Brice McAllister drawled. 'I always have to consult my diary before making appointments,' he added pointedly, that green gaze mocking her.

Sabina shot him a glaring look. Damn him, how dared he mock her when he knew she couldn't defend herself? Probably for exactly that reason! After all, there had to be some recompense for letting her off the hook so nobly!

'Three o'clock on Tuesday afternoon, then.' He nodded abruptly, obviously tiring of the game he was playing, anxious to be gone now as he took a card out of the pocket of his jacket.

Much as he had obviously enjoyed the game, damn him, Sabina inwardly acknowledged frustratedly. But what choice did she have now…?

'Fine,' she agreed abruptly, taking the card with his address printed on it, wishing she could somehow misplace it before next Tuesday. But at the same time knowing it would do her no good even if she did; that appointment might as well be set in stone as far as Richard was concerned!

Richard nodded. 'I have a meeting that afternoon, I'm afraid, Sabina, but I'll have Clive accompany you,' he assured her smilingly.

'Clive?' Brice McAllister repeated slowly. 'I have to tell you now, unlike Sabina, I do not like an audience while I work,' he bit out harshly.

Richard laughed dismissively. 'Clive is completely unobtrusive, I can assure you. But if it bothers you,' he added cajolingly as the other man still scowled, 'he can wait outside in the car.'

Brice nodded abruptly. 'It bothers me.'

No more than it *bothered* Sabina to think of spending that hour alone with him at his studio!

CHAPTER THREE

'WHAT do you know about the model Sabina?'

'Aha!' Chloe said with satisfaction as she put down her knife and fork to look across the luncheon table to Brice. 'I told Fergus, after you accompanied us to the fashion show last Saturday that there was something going on. So much for inviting me out to lunch to cheer me up while Fergus is away in Manchester at a book-signing!' she added teasingly.

Brice loved his cousin's wife dearly, looked on her as the younger sister he had never had, but sometimes...!

'There's nothing "going on", Chloe,' he told her dryly. 'I'm going to paint the woman. I just thought I should know something about her before I did.'

'Oh.' Chloe couldn't hide her disappointment at this explanation.

Brice gave a rueful shake of his head at her deflated expression. 'Just because you and Fergus are rapturously happy together—even more so since you knew about the expected baby—does not mean everyone else around you has to be in love too!'

'But wouldn't it be nice if you were?' Chloe came back undaunted.

'She's an engaged woman, Chloe,' he dismissed with amusement.

'But they don't seem in any hurry to get married,' she replied instantly. 'And Richard Latham is so much older than Sabina...'

Brice was all too well aware of that already...

'Nice' wasn't exactly how he would have described the

27

possibility of his falling in love. But he knew that his two cousins, Logan and Fergus, had found true love in the last year, and that they—and their wives!—would like nothing better than for Brice to join them in their obviously happy state. The only problem that he could see was that he hadn't yet found the woman that he could fall in love with!

The model Sabina certainly wasn't her. She was beautiful, yes. And from their meeting last Friday he knew that she was also completely natural and unaffected. He was also intrigued by her, found her engagement to a man so much her senior slightly odd, as he found the way she had the equivalent to a 'minder' accompany her wherever she went; because he had no doubt that the man Clive who would be driving her to his studio this afternoon was exactly that, no matter what guise he might otherwise be appearing under.

What Brice really wanted to know was, in view of David Latham's view of his uncle, was Sabina being protected on Richard's behalf, as a collector of priceless objects, or for some other reason…?

Which was why he had wondered, with Chloe being a fashion designer herself, with her own connections in the design and model world, if she knew anything about Sabina that might answer some of his questions for him. But the last thing he wanted was for Chloe to think he had a personal interest in Sabina!

'How is Fergus's latest book doing?' He decided to change the subject for a while; they could always come back to Sabina later.

'Number one in the hardback best-seller list after only two weeks,' Chloe told him with obvious pride. 'Have you read it?'

'Not yet.' He resumed eating his meal, knowing that he had successfully diverted Chloe's attention from possible wedding bells on his behalf. 'It's set in the fashion-designer world, isn't it?'

It was the perfect way to distract Chloe from the subject of Sabina, and for the next fifteen minutes they talked of Fergus's successful new book, then went on to discuss Chloe's father's return to politics, and now the government.

Anything but the beautiful model Sabina!

Because, as he'd talked to Chloe about everything else under the sun but Sabina, Brice had come to the realisation that his interest in her was personal!

She was deliberately cool and aloof, put up a barrier between herself and others—with the obvious exception of Richard Latham. And yet at the same time there was a vulnerability about her that seemed to be completely inexplicable.

Sabina was the world's top model, very beautiful, very much in demand, and very highly paid. Her earnings had to equal those of the highest paid actress in Hollywood. Which meant she had the money to be and do whatever she pleased. And yet…

It was that 'and yet' that intrigued Brice, that had him thinking about Sabina even when he wasn't aware he was doing it. He was becoming obsessed with her, he realised.

But this afternoon he hoped to go some way to solving the enigma that was Sabina Smith!

'Thanks for lunch, Brice.' Chloe reached up to kiss him on the cheek as they parted outside the restaurant. 'And good luck with Sabina this afternoon,' she added mischievously.

Brice gave a rueful shake of his head as he drove back to his home; he had no doubts that by this evening the whole family would know he had questioned Chloe concerning Sabina!

He arrived back at the house in plenty of time for their

three o'clock appointment. But three o'clock came and went, with no sign of Sabina.

She wasn't coming, damn it. After four days' wait, after all that anticipation, she wasn't coming!

Brice could feel the anger starting to build up inside him, having no doubt that Sabina had done this deliberately. He—

The doorbell rang.

It was three twenty-five, there had been no call to say she would be arriving late, but nevertheless Brice knew it was her. He schooled his features into showing none of his previous anger; that was probably what she expected, so she wouldn't get it!

'I'm so sorry I'm late,' Sabina was apologising profusely even as his housekeeper showed her into the studio a few minutes later. 'I had a photographic session for a magazine this morning, and, although they promised me faithfully that I would be finished by two o'clock, it ran over, and I—'

'You're here now,' Brice firmly cut into her lengthy explanation. Because he was sure, even from their brief acquaintance, that Sabina was not the effusive type, that she would never use half a dozen words when one would do. Which probably meant she was making this up as she went along! 'Have you had lunch?'

She blinked at this sudden change of subject. 'No...'

'Then can I offer you a sandwich or something?' He looked enquiringly at his housekeeper even as he made the offer.

'No, really,' Sabina refused before Mrs Potter could answer. 'I'll have something later,' she dismissed.

'Tea or coffee, then?' Brice offered smoothly.

God, she looked beautiful today, the clinging blue Lycra tee shirt, the same colour as her eyes, clinging in all the right places, as did the body-hugging black trousers she wore with it, her hair loose again today, a shining gold curtain down the length of her spine. Brice's fingers itched to take up paper and pencil and begin his sketches.

Sabina looked set to refuse again, and then obviously thought better of it. 'A coffee would be very nice, thank you.' She smiled warmly at the housekeeper.

'And how about Clive?' Brice couldn't resist asking, sure that the 'chauffeur' was even now sitting outside waiting to drive Sabina back to the home she shared with Richard Latham. As he had no doubt sat outside and waited for Sabina while she'd been in her photographic session this morning! 'Would he like a coffee too, do you think?' he added derisively.

Sabina's gaze narrowed as she looked across at him for several long, silent seconds. 'No, I'm sure Clive will be fine,' she finally answered slowly. 'I hope I'm not putting you to too much trouble,' she added warmly to the housekeeper.

Brice could see, as Mrs Potter left the studio with a smile on her face, that Sabina's apparently guileless charm had obviously worked its magic on her; he had no doubt that there would be more than a cup of coffee on the tray the housekeeper brought back in a few minutes.

'Where do you want me?'

Now there was a leading question if ever he had heard one, Brice acknowledged derisively, sure that most men wouldn't care 'where' with Sabina, as long as they had her!

Brice's outward expression remained impassive. 'The couch, I think,' he answered consideringly. 'To start with. I'm really not sure what I'm going to do with this yet,' he added frowningly. How could he possibly do justice to such a beauty as Sabina's...?

There was no doubting her surface beauty, but there was so much more to her than that, a naturalness that owed nothing to powder and paint, an inner Sabina that he needed to reach too. And he was determined, no matter what barriers she might choose to put up, that he would reach *that* Sabina!

Sabina moved to sit on the couch, the May sun shining in brightly through the windows that made up one complete wall of Brice McAllister's studio. The garden outside was a blaze of spring flowers, and just the sight of that mixture of bright blossoms lightened Sabina's spirit.

'Do you do the gardening yourself?' she asked interestedly.

'Sorry?'

She turned back to look at Brice McAllister, only to find he was already engrossed in the sketch-pad resting on his knee as he sat across the room from her. 'I didn't realise you had already started,' she murmured slightly resentfully, knowing she had been caught off guard as she'd looked out at the beauty of the garden.

'Only roughly,' he dismissed, giving her his full attention now, looking very relaxed in blue denims and a black tee shirt. 'And yes, I look after the garden myself, It's often a welcome relief after being in my studio for hours. Do you garden?'

Her expression became wistful. 'I used to.'

'Before pressures of work made it impossible,' Brice McAllister guessed lightly.

A shutter came down over her eyes. 'Something like that,' she answered noncommittally.

The fact that she no longer gardened had nothing to do with work commitments, and everything to do with the fact that she no longer lived alone in her little cottage. But she was not about to explain that to Brice McAllister.

She was only here at all today under protest, because last Friday she had been given no choice but to agree to the appointment. Part of her knew that she probably also owed Brice a thank-you for not telling Richard how she had been avoiding his phone calls all week. But there was something inside her that wouldn't let her say the words...

"'Something like that"?' Brice repeated softly.

Sabina shifted uncomfortably. 'I'm not sure I'm going to be any good at this; I'm simply not good at sitting still.' She grimaced.

He nodded. 'Stand up and move around if you prefer it; I'm not sure sitting down is the right pose for you anyway,' he added frowningly.

Sabina wondered as she stood up to move restlessly about the room exactly what pose he did think was right for her?

Brice McAllister's studio was a cluttered and yet somehow orderly room, canvases stacked against the walls, paints, pencils, paper, all neatly stored on open shelves, with the minimum amount of furniture; just the chair he sat in, a large, paint-daubed table, and the couch Sabina had been sitting on.

'Here we are.' Mrs Potter came back in with a laden tray, putting it down on the table, sandwiches and a fruit cake also on the tray.

'Thank you,' Sabina told the other woman warmly.

'Help yourself,' Brice McAllister invited dryly once his housekeeper had left the room.

She poured the tea into two cups before helping herself to one of the chicken sandwiches; she hadn't thought she was hungry, but one bite of the delicious sandwich told her that she was.

'Do you often miss out on lunch?' Brice McAllister watched her with brooding eyes.

Sabina shrugged. 'Sometimes. But I usually make up for it later,' she assured him dryly. 'I don't starve myself, if that's what you're thinking; I'm naturally like this.' She indicated the slenderness of her figure.

'And very nice it is too.' He nodded. 'When's the wedding?'

Sabina blinked at the sudden change of subject. 'Sorry…?'

'Richard implied your portrait is a wedding present to himself.' Brice shrugged. 'I was merely wondering how soon I have to finish it,' he added derisively.

She frowned. 'I think you must have misunderstood him.' It had never even been discussed between them that their 'understanding' might lead to marriage…

'No?' He raised dark brows. 'Richard gave me the impression it was imminent.'

'Did he?' she returned evenly, equally sure he must have misunderstood Richard.

'I thought so,' Brice continued determinedly. 'There's rather a large difference in your ages, isn't there?'

Her cheeks flushed resentfully. What business was it of this man if there was an age difference between herself and her fiancé? Absolutely none, came the unqualified answer!

'Spring and autumn,' Brice added derisively.

Her mouth twisted. 'At twenty-five I'm hardly spring— summer would be more appropriate,' she bit out shortly. 'And surely age is irrelevant in this day and age?' she added challengingly.

'Is it?' he returned softly.

Sabina frowned across at him, more disturbed by what he had said than she cared to admit. She and Richard were friends, nothing more; Brice must have misunderstood Richard! Mustn't he…?

'I thought I came here so you could sketch me, Mr McAllister—not question me about my personal life!' she snapped agitatedly.

'The name is Brice,' he told her smoothly.

'I prefer Mr McAllister,' she said tautly. What she really preferred was to keep this man very much at a distance!

He gave an unperturbed shrug. 'Whatever. Could you stand over by the fireplace?' he bit out curtly, once again frowning down at his sketch-pad.

Almost as if that very personal conversation had never taken place, Sabina fumed inwardly as she moved to stand beside the unlit fireplace.

'Yes,' Brice breathed his satisfaction with the pose. 'The clothes are all wrong, of course—not that you don't look lovely in them,' he added as she raised her brows. 'They just aren't right for the way I want to paint you.'

'And what way is that?' Sabina rasped impatiently.

He didn't answer her, frowning across the room at her in between making rapid strokes with his pencil on the pad in front of him.

Sabina remained standing exactly as she was, recognising that transfixed look from some of her photographic sessions; a master was at work, and for the moment she, as a person, did not exist.

Which was fine with her. She was here under protest, and the last thing she wanted was any more personal conversations with Brice McAllister while she was here. Especially of the kind they had just had.

'Will there have to be much of this?' she finally felt compelled to ask him an hour later. The fireplace was really rather nice, but after looking at it for the last hour she definitely knew it didn't hold much scope for the imagination!

Brice looked up at her frowningly, his thoughts obviously still engrossed in his sketching. 'Much of what?'

'These sittings—or, in this case, standings,' she added wryly. 'Will I need to do many of them?'

He put the sketch-pad down on the table beside him, flexing stiff shoulder muscles as he did so.

He really was a very handsome man, Sabina acknowledged grudgingly. Those dark, brooding good looks were almost Byronic, that over-long dark hair giving him a rakishly gypsy appearance. Although Sabina was sure the romantic Byron had never quite had that totally assessing male look in his eyes. Deep green eyes that even now were trying to look past her façade of politeness to the inner Sabina!

'Why?' he finally drawled softly.

She shrugged. 'As I've already explained, I'm—'

'Rather busy,' he finished derisively. 'Yes, you have explained that. Several times, as I recall,' he added mockingly before picking up his cup and drinking the now cold tea in one swallow. 'The question is, why are you so busy?' He looked at her with narrowed eyes. 'As I understand it, you've been one of the top models in the world—if not the top model in the world,' he allowed mockingly, 'for the last five years. Why do you need to keep working at the pace that you do?'

Because work stopped her from thinking, from remembering, meant she was too tired at night to do anything more than fall into bed and go to sleep!

But none of those thoughts betrayed themselves in the calmness of her expression. 'So that I *remain* one of the top models in the world,' she replied dryly.

Brice pursed his mouth. 'And is that important to you?'

Her cheeks became flushed at the mockery in his tone. 'Is it important to you to be one of the world's most sought-after artists?' she returned caustically, deeply resenting the slight condescension towards her career that she sensed in his tone.

Okay, so it didn't need great intelligence to initially become a model, just the right look, and a certain amount of

luck, but it certainly took more than those things to remain
one. She worked hard at what she did, never gave less than
her best, and she deeply resented his implication that it
should be otherwise. She had always regarded herself as
something of an artist too, in her own way.

'*Touché,*' he allowed dryly. 'I just can't imagine doing
what you do, day in and day out.' He shrugged.

Sabina narrowed cornflower-blue eyes on him. 'Are you
meaning to be insulting, Mr McAllister, or does it just
come naturally?' she said slowly.

He grinned unabashedly. 'A little of both, probably.'

She shook her head, incredulous at his arrogance. 'You
just don't care, do you?' she murmured slowly.

He looked puzzled. 'About what?'

'About anything,' she realised in wonder.

How she wished she still had that tolerantly amused outlook to life, that she could laugh at herself as well as other
people. But she knew that she didn't. That she never would
have again, thanks to—

No, she wouldn't think of that. Couldn't think of that.

'I think it's time I was going,' she decided abruptly,
glancing pointedly at the gold watch on her wrist. An engagement present from Richard. That, and his diamond
engagement ring, were the only two pieces of jewellery
she ever wore.

Brice McAllister was watching her consideringly, head
tilted slightly to one side, green gaze narrowed speculatively. 'Why?' he finally challenged.

It was a challenge Sabina easily picked up on. And
chose to ignore. 'Because I have somewhere else to go,'
she told him determinedly.

'Home to Richard?' he taunted softly, standing up
slowly, his sheer size totally dominating the room.

Sabina took a step back, suddenly finding the room oppressively small. She also found herself backed up against the unlit fireplace.

Brice walked slowly towards her, his narrowed gaze not leaving her face. He stopped about a foot away, that gaze searching now as he continued to look at her.

For the second time since she had met him Sabina found she couldn't breathe.

This close to, she could feel the male warmth of him, could smell the slight tang of the aftershave he wore, could see every pore and hair on the darkness of his skin. But it was none of those things that constricted her breathing. She knew it was his sheer physical closeness that did that.

She swallowed convulsively. 'I really do have to go,' she told him breathlessly.

Brice looked at her steadily. 'So what's stopping you?' he prompted huskily.

Her legs, for one thing. They refused to move. In fact, she felt so weak at the knees they were only just succeeding in supporting her. She felt like a mesmerised rabbit caught on the road in the glare of car headlights, incapable of movement, even in the face of such obvious danger.

And Brice McAllister, as she had half guessed on their very first meeting, been even more convinced of it at their second, was exactly that—dangerous!

She moistened suddenly dry lips. 'If you would just move out of my way...?'

He stepped slightly to one side. 'Be my guest,' he invited softly.

Sabina forced her legs to move, quickly, determinedly, crossing to the door, putting as much distance between herself and Brice McAllister as was possible in the confines of the studio.

'I'll call you.'

Sabina turned sharply as he spoke, her trembling hand already on the door-handle. 'Excuse me?'

Brice raised dark brows, his mouth twisted in mocking amusement. 'I said, I'll call you. For your next sitting,' he explained derisively as she still looked totally blank.

Get a grip, Sabina, she ordered herself sternly. What had really happened just now—Brice McAllister had stood what she considered was too close to her? So what? And yet she knew that wasn't really all that had happened, that there had been a frisson of awareness between the two of them that she wished weren't there...

'Perhaps you would do me the courtesy of taking my call this time?' Brice prompted confidently.

Colour darkened her cheeks at his certainty she had no choice but to do exactly that. 'If I happen to be at home,' she bit out harshly.

He shrugged. 'If you aren't, I'm sure that Richard and I can sort out a time between the two of us,' he drawled softly.

Sabina's eyes narrowed. 'Contrary to what you may have assumed otherwise, Mr McAllister—I make my own appointments,' she snapped coldly.

Once again he gave that humourless smile. 'That wasn't my impression at our last meeting.'

Because at the time she had been at the disadvantage of not wanting him to tell Richard she had been avoiding his telephone calls for the past week!

She looked at him consideringly for several long seconds. 'You know, Mr McAllister,' she finally said softly, 'I really don't give a damn what was or wasn't your *impression* at our last meeting,' she told him scornfully. 'In fact, nothing about you is of the least interest to me,' she added scathingly.

He raised dark brows. 'No?'

'No!' she confirmed hardly. 'Goodbye, Mr McAllister.' She wrenched the door open.

'*Au revoir*, surely, Sabina...?' he taunted softly.

Sabina didn't even turn and acknowledge the obvious challenge, striding briskly out of the room, closing the front door softly behind her as she left.

It wasn't until she was safely ensconced in the back seat of the car, Clive driving back to Richard's house, that she allowed free rein to her feelings.

She didn't like the way Brice McAllister looked at her. Didn't like the way he had of talking to her on a very personal level. Didn't like him near her. In fact, she just didn't like him!

And she had no idea how she was going to achieve it, but she had no intention of being alone with Brice in his studio ever again!

CHAPTER FOUR

BRICE cursed himself, for what had to be the hundredth time in a week, for the way he had behaved with Sabina last Tuesday.

He had already seen the fear and apprehension in her eyes at their first meeting, had realised she was inwardly like a startled fawn getting ready for flight, and yet some devil had driven him on to try and get a reaction from her, to taunt and mock her in an effort to get behind the cool façade she liked to present to the world at large.

But all he had succeeded in doing was totally alienating her.

Oh, it hadn't resulted in her refusing to take his calls this time. She had taken all four of them—she had simply come up with a legitimate excuse for every suggestion he'd come up with for a second sitting!

And what had she left him with? She could spare him one hour this morning, but it would have to be at home. Probably with the quietly watchful Richard in attendance!

As he was only at the sketching stage, Brice hadn't been able to come up with a good reason why he shouldn't be the one to go to her home. But that didn't mean he liked it...

Although he had to admit a few minutes later, when he was shown into the sitting-room where Sabina waited—alone—that she was much more relaxed in her own surroundings. In fact, she was the epitome of the gracious hostess, smiling at him politely as she offered him tea or coffee. Both of which he refused.

She looked the part too, in a cream silk blouse and pencil-slim black skirt, the latter finishing just above her knee, her hair gathered up in a neat chignon at the back of her head. Altogether, she looked nothing like the woman Brice wanted to capture on canvas!

'Practising for domesticity?' he drawled mockingly.

He had been determined to be totally professional today, to put Sabina at her ease. But somehow he couldn't help himself; this new Sabina brought back that devil inside him even more strongly than the other one. She was playing a part, adopting a role—and Brice didn't doubt for a moment that it was for his benefit. Only confirming for him that he really had struck a sensitive nerve with his behaviour the previous week!

She smiled across at him coolly. 'You were right last week, Brice—being rude does seem to come naturally to you.'

Which was his cue to apologise. But he couldn't do that, either. Something about this woman made him want to grip her by the shoulders and shake her, to see her laugh, or cry, to show some impulsive emotion. Which would probably result in him being thrown out of here on his ear!

He shrugged. 'Merely being observant,' he dismissed lightly. 'I'm sorry, but your hair has to come down, at least,' he added frowningly, having settled himself down in a chair with his notepad and pencil.

She shook her head. 'I'm afraid I'm going out to lunch immediately after this, and I won't have time to redo my hair,' she refused.

Brice bit back his irritation; she really was only giving him the hour! 'You look as if you're about to meet your bank manager,' he rasped insultingly.

Sabina's gaze didn't waver from his for a moment, although there was, he thought, the briefest flare of anger in those deep blue depths.

'My mother, actually,' she drawled coolly.

Brice raised dark brows. 'Her daughter is the most famous model in the world—and she likes you to look like this?' He couldn't hide his incredulity. And so much for his arrogance in assuming she had dressed in this way as a barrier against him!

Sabina bristled resentfully. 'What's wrong with the way I look?'

It would be easier—and quicker—to say what was right with it. Nothing! Oh, she looked elegant enough, but that hairstyle and those clothes took away all her personality. She certainly had none of the provocative beauty of the model Sabina at this moment.

'My mother has lived in Scotland since my father died, so I only see her a couple of times a year,' she told him defensively. 'She's rather—conventional, in her outlook,' Sabina continued abruptly when he still didn't reply.

Brice's gaze narrowed. 'In what way?'

Sabina shrugged. 'She and my father were very career-minded, both teachers of history at university level. I don't think they ever intended having children, but accidents happen.' Sabina grimaced. 'They were rather older than most parents when I was born, my mother forty-one, my father forty-six. Although I think my father coped with parenthood rather better than my mother did,' she said frowningly. 'But then, I suppose he didn't have to put his own career on hold for five years, until I was old enough to go to school,' she added fairly.

Considering this was the most Sabina had ever spoken to him, Brice could only think she had to be as nervous of this second sitting as he was.

'You must have been rather a shock to them,' Brice said ruefully.

In more ways than one. Suddenly being presented with a very young baby must have been shock enough, but how on earth had her aged parents coped with Sabina's unmistakable beauty? She must have looked like an angel when she was a little girl.

'Yes,' she acknowledged wistfully. 'It was a strange childhood,' she admitted abruptly.

Probably a very lonely one too, Brice realised frowningly. Something he found difficult to contemplate. He had grown up in a young, fun-loving family, and when he hadn't been with his parents he had been in Scotland, with his grandfather, and his two cousins, Logan and Fergus. He had never particularly thought about it before, but his own childhood couldn't have been more perfect.

'Which one of your parents do you take after?' he probed interestedly, going carefully so as not to break the spell; he had a feeling that Sabina rarely spoke of her parents and her childhood, and that to draw her attention to it now would only result in her clamming up again.

Sabina gave the ghost of a smile. 'My father.' That smile faded almost as soon as it appeared. 'He died five years ago,' she added flatly.

And her mother had lived in Scotland since that time.

'I'm sorry.' And he was. Even from the little she had said, it was obvious Sabina had been much closer to her father than her mother.

And perhaps that closeness to her father, and his death five years ago, explained the reason for her engagement now to a man so much her senior?

Sabina shrugged. 'He had been ill with cancer for some time; it was a welcome release for him.' She spoke unemotionally. 'But I've always regretted that he wasn't there to see me get my own degree in history. Oh, yes, Brice—' she smiled at his obviously surprised expression '—I went to university. I haven't always been a full-time model,' she added derisively, for his derogatory remarks about her chosen career the previous week.

And her derision was well deserved, Brice acknowledged inwardly. He had been scathing and rude about her career, without really knowing anything about this woman; no wonder she looked on him as an inconvenient intrusion!

Sabina's humour faded, her expression becoming non-committal once again. 'My mother—obviously—is a great believer in further education for women, believes women should have as many choices in life as they can possibly achieve.' Her mouth twisted ruefully. 'I don't think she's too impressed with the fact that, for the moment, I've chosen modelling.'

'But it is obviously by choice.' Brice shrugged, frowning suddenly. 'And if your mother is so conventional in her outlook, what does she make of your living here with Richard so openly?'

He hadn't even finished saying the words before knowing he had just made a terrible mistake. And the truth of the matter was, he wasn't interested in how Sabina's mother felt about her living arrangements; he wanted to know the answer to this particular question himself.

Because he found the idea of Sabina sharing Richard Latham's house, Richard Latham's bed, completely unacceptable.

Sabina had stood up abruptly as soon as he'd asked the question, blue eyes blazing angrily across the room at him now. 'You're being extremely personal, Mr McAllister!' she snapped, two bright spots of angry colour in her cheeks.

And her anger, Brice realised, wasn't all directed towards him; she had also realised, having been drawn into an unguarded conversation about her parents, that she had actually left herself open to Brice's overfamiliarity. And she was obviously furious with herself because of it.

Brice remained seated. 'Talking of Richard...where is your fiancé today?' he enquired mildly; he really had expected the other man to be here today. If only to keep an eye on one of his 'priceless possessions'!

'He's in New York until tomorrow,' Sabina bit out economically.

'In that case—will you have dinner with me this evening?' Brice heard himself asking.

And then kicked himself. What on earth did he think he was doing? Sabina was an engaged woman. More important, she had given no indication whatsoever that she was in the least interested in spending time in his company. In fact, the opposite seemed true!

Sabina looked as stunned by the invitation as Brice felt at having made it.

The angry colour had faded from her cheeks, leaving them pale as alabaster, her eyes dark and unfathomable as she stared at him uncomprehendingly. Almost as if she didn't believe what she had just heard.

As if to taunt Brice for his audacity, the diamond ring Sabina wore on her left hand winked and shone in the sunlight shining in through the large bay windows. Richard Latham's ring…

Brice held his hands up in apology. 'It was just a thought. A bad one,' he accepted dryly as she continued to stare at him. 'But it was only a dinner invitation, Sabina,' he continued angrily as she stood unmoving across the room. 'Not an improper suggestion!'

She swallowed hard before drawing in a ragged breath. 'I didn't think—' She broke off as a brief knock sounded on the door. 'Come in,' she invited huskily, obviously relieved at the housekeeper's interruption as she turned to smile at the older woman.

Brice's relief was of another kind—the housekeeper had probably just delayed him receiving a verbal slap in the face!

'You asked me to bring the post straight in when it arrived, Miss Sabina.' Mrs Clark held out the silver tray on which she carried at least half a dozen letters.

'Thank you.' Sabina's second smile, as she took the letters, looked rather strained to Brice as he watched her from across the room.

As, indeed, it probably was! Damn it, what did he think he was doing, inviting Sabina out to dinner? She hadn't liked him very much to start with; now she was going to think even less of him!

What on earth had prompted him to make such an invitation? Sabina had gone out of her way to show him she had no desire to be in his company, for any reason, so why put himself in this ridiculous position? Probably because of that complete aversion she made no effort to hide, he accepted ruefully.

Not that he expected every woman he met to fall at his feet; no matter what Sabina might think to the contrary, he really wasn't that arrogant. But he didn't usually have the effect of dislike at first sight, either!

He had had his share of relationships over the years, some of them very enjoyable, some of them not so much fun, but he could never before remember a woman taking an instant dislike to him in the way that Sabina had...

Contrarily, it had only succeeded in making him more interested in Sabina!

The housekeeper having left the room now, Brice stood up abruptly. 'I think we may as well call it a day for now,' he bit out harshly. 'You obviously—' He came to an abrupt halt, Sabina having turned sharply towards him as he spoke, dropping the letters from her hand onto the carpeted floor as a consequence.

Damn it, was he really that much of a monster to her after that stupid dinner invitation that just the sound of his voice now took her back into that 'startled fawn' mode? If so he—

'What is it?' he prompted sharply as Sabina rose slowly from picking up the dropped letters, her face not just white now but a ghastly grey. 'Sabina...?' He moved abruptly to her side, grasping the tops of her arms as his gaze quickly searched the haunting beauty of her face. She looked as if she was about to faint! 'Here, sit down.' He put her down in one of the armchairs before striding over to the tray of drinks on the side and pouring a large amount of brandy into a glass.

'No, thanks,' Sabina refused huskily as she looked up and saw what he was doing. 'I don't think my mother will be too impressed if I turn up for lunch smelling of brandy!' she attempted to tease.

Brice knew the remark for exactly what it was—an attempt to divert his attention from the fact that she looked so awful. It failed!

He frowned down at her, feeling in need himself now of the brandy in the glass he still held. 'Is the idea of dinner with me really so repugnant to you…?' He couldn't believe his invitation had had this much of an effect on her.

'Sorry?' Sabina frowned up at him, obviously confused by the question.

Which led Brice to wonder if it had been his invitation that had brought about this transformation in her.

But if it wasn't his invitation that had caused her to look so ill so suddenly, what—? He looked down at the letters she had just picked up, most of them in her right hand, while her left hand tightly clutched an envelope of pale green. Gripped it so tightly, in fact, that the envelope was crushed in her fingers until the knuckles showed white…!

Brice looked down at her searchingly. She hadn't had time to open any of the letters, and yet just the sight of that pale green envelope had been enough to drain her face of all colour!

'Sabina—'

She stood up abruptly. 'Of course the idea of dinner with you isn't repugnant to me,' she told him with forced lightness, while at the same time totally avoiding his gaze. 'In fact, it sounds a wonderful idea,' she accepted.

That wasn't the impression she had given before the housekeeper had arrived with the mail; in fact Brice was positive Sabina had had every intention of turning down his invitation until that moment.

But for some reason she recognised that particular green envelope, knew who the letter was from without even opening it. And it had disturbed her enough for her to want to accept Brice's dinner invitation…

Curiouser, and curiouser.

'Fine,' he said before she had chance to change her mind. 'I'll call for you at about seven-thirty, if that's okay?'

'Perfect,' she agreed quickly, obviously anxious for him to leave now.

So that she could read the letter in that pale green envelope…?

His mouth twisted ruefully. 'Shall I book the table for three—or will you be giving Clive the evening off?' He certainly didn't relish the idea of sitting down to dinner with Sabina under the other man's watchful gaze, sitting outside the restaurant or otherwise!

Sabina gave him a reproachful glance. 'I'm sure I can manage without Clive for one evening,' she bit out tersely before glancing at her wrist-watch. 'I'm sorry we don't seem to have got very far this morning, Brice, but I'm afraid I have to go now.' Her obvious need for him to leave now became even more intense. 'Otherwise I'll be late for my luncheon appointment.'

'And that would displease your mother,' Brice drawled. 'And we mustn't have that, must we?' he acknowledged derisively.

But he really shouldn't complain, he berated himself as he picked up his things and prepared to leave; he had achieved much more this morning than he had expected to.

Sabina had told him more about her family than he had ever thought she would, her older parents, her conventional mother who now lived in Scotland—which part? he couldn't help wondering, with his own family connections in Scotland—her closeness to her father, his death five years ago.

Yes, he had learnt all of that about her today, and it was so much more than he had expected. But what he really wanted to know was, what was it about the letter she had received that had so upset her...? Because he was more and more convinced that it had been the letter and not him that had brought about that transformation in Sabina. Damn it, she had been so anxious to get rid of him after receiving it that she had even accepted his dinner invitation!

Maybe over dinner this evening—without the watchdog, Clive—he would have a chance to ask her about the letter in the pale green envelope...?

'Call for you, Miss Sabina,' Mrs Clark informed her later that day when Sabina picked up the telephone extension in her bedroom. 'It's Mr Latham,' she added lightly.

Richard...!

'Thank you, Mrs Clark.' Sabina eagerly took the call. After the day she had just had, she was longing to hear the normality of his voice! 'Richard,' she greeted warmly. 'How are you? Is everything okay? There's no delay in your coming home tomorrow, is there?' she added worriedly.

'Hey, one question at a time,' Richard's reassuringly familiar voice teased her indulgently. 'I'm fine. And everything is okay for my return tomorrow. I have a business meeting soon, but I just thought I would give you a call first to see how your week has been.'

Until earlier today it had been fine. She had been so busy that she hadn't really had the time to even think about the fact that Richard was in New York for four days. But that had all changed this morning. And now she just wanted him to come home!

'Fine,' she answered dismissively. 'Very busy work-wise, of course.'

'And what are you doing this evening?' Richard asked interestedly.

Well, so far she had showered, and washed her hair before drying it, had applied her make-up, put on a black sheath dress, and now she was sitting here in her bedroom waiting for Brice McAllister to arrive to take her out to dinner.

But somehow she knew she couldn't tell Richard quite so bluntly that she was going out to dinner with the other man.

She had had every intention of refusing Brice McAllister's dinner invitation, but then Mrs Clark had brought in the post, and thrown Sabina into complete confusion. So much so that, in an effort to get Brice to leave, she had accepted the dinner invitation, after all!

But quite how she told Richard about that she didn't really know...

She winced. 'Actually, I'm seeing Brice McAllister this evening,' she began reluctantly.

'That's good,' Richard told her approvingly. 'How are the sittings coming along? Has the great man come down out of his ivory tower now and realised that you're the most gorgeous creature on two legs and that he just has to paint you?'.

'Not exactly,' she answered dryly, at the same time knowing that Richard had completely misunderstood her reason for seeing Brice this evening, that he believed it to be for another sitting.

Not that there was anything wrong with her having dinner with another man; she had done it dozens of times in the course of her modelling career. She just knew that dinner with Brice McAllister didn't quite come into that category...

She drew in a deep breath. 'Actually, Richard—'

'Just a minute, Sabina,' he cut in apologetically. 'I have a call on my other line.'

Sabina waited patiently while he took the other call, but the longer she waited, the more her courage was failing her. She had no doubt that Richard would have no problem with her meeting Brice McAllister for a sitting, but having dinner with the other man—with not a sketch-book or pencil in sight—was something else completely.

She wasn't altogether happy with the arrangement herself, but, having once accepted the dinner invitation, she hadn't felt she could phone Brice McAllister and cancel it. Part of the reason for that, she knew, was that Brice McAllister was sure to know exactly why she had cancelled it. And he seemed to find enough reason to mock her already, without adding to it!

'Sorry about that, Sabina.' Richard came back on the line. 'My business appointment just arrived, so I have to go. I'll call you later this evening if I get a chance, okay?'

No, it wasn't okay! What if Richard telephoned while she was still out and Mrs Clark told him she was out to dinner with the other man? And yet, at the same time, she knew this wasn't the right time to talk to Richard about it, either; he was obviously in a hurry to get to his appointment, meaning she wouldn't be able to explain things to him properly before he had to rush off.

'I was actually thinking of having an early night,' she told him instead. 'But I'll meet you at the airport tomorrow, anyway.' When she would definitely explain about seeing Brice this evening.

'There's no need for you to come all the way out to Heathrow,' Richard assured her lightly. 'Just send Clive with the car.'

As far as Sabina was concerned, there was every need. Besides, the privacy in the back of the car would give her a chance to talk to him on the journey home.

'I'm not doing anything tomorrow, and I would really like the trip out,' she assured him.

'Okay, fine,' Richard answered distractedly. 'I'll see you then,' he added before ringing off.

Wonderful! Not only was she having dinner with a man she would rather not spend time alone with, but she had also just lied to her fiancé about it.

What was it about Brice McAllister that made her so nervous she felt compelled to do such a thing?

Those green eyes that looked directly into her soul, came the instant answer to that question.

Those deceptively sleepy green eyes actually missed nothing, Sabina was sure. He was completely aware of her aversion to sitting for him. Her nervousness about this morning's sitting had resulted in her talking far too much. Ordinarily a very reserved person, she still couldn't believe she had talked to Brice about her family in the way that she had this morning.

She was also sure Brice hadn't missed her reaction this morning to the arrival in the post of that green envelope...

It had been three weeks since she'd last received one, the longest time ever, lulling her into a completely false sense of security, she now realised. Her reaction to receiving one this morning had been all the stronger because of that.

And Brice had seen that response.

Consequently, Sabina had been in a very agitated state by the time she'd met her mother for lunch. So much so that she'd almost missed what was different about this half-yearly visit to London by her mother.

'Have you and Richard set a date for your wedding yet, Sabina?' her mother enquired lightly as they both ate a prawn salad accompanied by a glass of white wine.

Sabina almost choked as she took a sip of that white wine. Why was it that everyone—Brice McAllister, most recently—seemed to be showing an interest in exactly when she and Richard were going to be married?

'Not yet,' she answered noncommittally, not even her mother having any idea of the almost businesslike arrangement of the engagement. 'We aren't in any rush,' she added to take any sting out of her words, watching as her mother carefully replaced her own wineglass on the table after taking a small sip.

Everything about her mother was controlled and careful, from her coiffured blonde head down to her moderately heeled black shoes, the latter worn to complement the black suit and cream blouse she was wearing today.

Sabina loved her mother dearly, had always admired her—she had just never been able to talk to her! Which was one of the reasons these half-yearly lunches together were such a trial. To both of them, Sabina felt sure.

'I only asked because I'm thinking of taking a short holiday early in the autumn, and I wouldn't like it to clash with your wedding,' her mother continued evenly.

'That will make a lovely change.' Sabina nodded approvingly; her mother seemed to lead a very uneventful life at her cottage home in Scotland. 'Are you going anywhere nice?' she added interestedly, relieved to have a neutral topic they could converse on.

'I haven't decided yet,' her mother dismissed with a brief smile. 'I—I'm going with a friend,' she added awkwardly, her gaze suddenly not quite meeting Sabina's. 'We thought perhaps Paris for a few days might be rather fun.'

Sabina frowned across the table at her mother. Fun? It wasn't a word she usually associated with her carefully controlled mother. There was something—

'Do I know this friend?' she prompted lightly, suddenly knowing, from the blush slowly creeping up her mother's cheeks, that she didn't.

Because the 'friend' was male!

Quite why Sabina should feel so shaken at the knowledge, she wasn't sure. Her father had been dead for five years, her mother was only in her mid-sixties, and still a very attractive woman; tiny, her figure slim, shoulder-length blonde hair always neatly styled, the beauty of her face barely lined. But somehow the thought of her mother going away on 'a short holiday', to romantic Paris of all places, with a man other than Sabina's father, threw her into total confusion.

All in all, she decided now as she gave one last check of her appearance in the mirror before going downstairs to wait for Brice McAllister's arrival, this had not been a good day.

And she very much doubted dinner with Brice McAllister was going to make it any better!

CHAPTER FIVE

IT HADN'T needed a mind-reader, when Brice had arrived at the house to pick Sabina up half an hour ago, to know that she wished she were spending her evening in any other way than having dinner with him!

Even now they had arrived at the quietly elegant restaurant, Sabina was anything but relaxed. It was up to Brice to see that she became so. Because she might not have been looking forward to seeing him this evening, but he certainly didn't feel the same way about spending the evening with her!

Sabina intrigued him. Her beauty was mesmerising, very much so in the simple figure-hugging black dress she wore tonight, everyone in the restaurant turning to stare at her admiringly a few minutes ago as the two of them had walked to their table. But it was the woman behind that beauty that interested Brice too, the intelligence behind those deep blue eyes.

Wary blue eyes. Which was why Brice had decided, before coming out this evening, rightly or wrongly, that he wouldn't pursue the subject of her reaction to the arrival of the letter in the green envelope. Not that he intended forgetting about it, but if he pressed Sabina for an explanation this evening he probably wouldn't see her for dust. Also, a part of him knew that she was half expecting him to ask her about it, and, perversely, he had decided not to do so!

'How did your lunch go with your mother?' he asked lightly instead as they perused the menus.

'Fine,' she answered brightly.

But Brice wasn't fooled by that dismissive façade, had

seen the shadow that had entered her eyes at the mention of her mother. He had what he considered a pretty healthy relationship with his own mother—they were good enough friends that he didn't interfere in her life as long as she didn't interfere in his.

But he knew from the little Sabina had told him of her own mother that the two of them didn't have that sort of relationship.

He gave Sabina a considering look. 'Sure?'

She frowned across at him. 'Of course I—' She broke off with a sigh. 'No, not really,' she conceded ruefully, fidgeting with her wineglass. 'It wasn't like our usual lunches together at all.'

Brice put down his menu, already knowing what he was going to choose, having been to this restaurant many times before. 'In what way?'

She shrugged. 'It seems that my mother has a boyfriend,' she disclosed reluctantly. 'Well…not a boyfriend, exactly.' She grimaced at the term. 'But there is a man she intends going on holiday with to Paris in the autumn,' she added frowningly.

'Isn't that good?' But Brice already knew that in Sabina's eyes it wasn't, could hear the underlying strain in her voice. 'She's been on her own for five years, and she must only be in her mid-sixties…?' Sabina was only aged in her mid-twenties, and she had said her mother had been forty-one when Sabina had been born…

'Sixty-six,' Sabina confirmed, giving a self-conscious grimace. 'I'm being selfish, aren't I? I've just never thought of my mother in that way.' She shook her head.

'Obviously this man has,' he said without thinking—and then wished he hadn't when he saw the disconcerted look on Sabina's face. 'I'm sorry, Sabina,' he at once apologised. 'It's just—'

'I know, I know,' she cut in self-derisively, taking a sip of the white wine Brice had chosen for them to enjoy before their meal. 'I really don't know why I'm even bothering to tell you this.' She gave an embarrassed laugh. 'I'm sure you can't be in the least interested.'

Now there she was completely wrong; as Brice was only too aware, everything about this woman interested him! In fact, he couldn't remember being this interested in a woman for years...

'But I am,' he assured her softly.

She shook her head. 'Please forget I ever mentioned it. I'm being silly.'

And Brice knew she was also unhappy with herself for having spoken to him about it!

'What is it you find strange about the situation?' he persisted lightly. 'The fact that your mother may have found a man she obviously enjoys spending time with? Or the fact that it isn't your father?' he added gently, already knowing it was probably the latter.

'Stupid, isn't it?' Sabina murmured self-disgustedly.

'Not in the least,' Brice instantly assured her. 'I don't think you've met my cousin Logan and his wife Darcy...?'

Sabina shook her head, her puzzled expression showing she had no idea where this conversation could possibly be going. 'I believe they were at the Hamilton party the night we first met, but I wasn't introduced to them, no.'

'Well, the two of them fell in love with each other while they were trying to prevent a relationship between Darcy's father and Logan's mother.' And a merry old tangle it had been at the time, as Brice easily recalled.

But he could see he definitely had Sabina's attention now.

'What happened to the father and mother?' she prompted curiously.

Perhaps, he realised too late, making that particular comparison hadn't been such a good idea, after all! 'They were married about a month before Logan and Darcy,' he revealed reluctantly as he realised that was probably the last thing Sabina wanted to hear.

'Oh,' she concluded flatly.

But Brice could see her thoughts were still preoccupied as they ordered their meal. She really didn't diet to keep that wonderful figure, ordering asparagus smothered in butter as a starter, followed by steak in Stilton sauce accompanied by Lyonnaise potatoes as her main course.

'I'll probably have something gooily chocolate as dessert too,' she apologised as she saw him watching her indulgently once the waiter had departed with their order.

Brice wasn't complaining; after years of having dinner with women who chose the items on the menu with the least calories, and then proceeded to only pick at even those when they arrived, it was a refreshing change to be with a woman who obviously enjoyed her food.

'Be my guest,' he invited warmly. 'You're just the sort of customer Daniel loves to cook for,' he assured her.

'You know the chef here?' She took another sip of her white wine.

Brice gave a rueful grimace as he realised he had done it again. 'Would you believe Chef Simon is Darcy's father?'

Sabina laughed huskily. 'I'd believe it.' She smiled. 'He's married to the actress Margaret Fraser, isn't he?'

'My Aunt Meg.' Brice nodded. 'They're very happy together.'

'I said I believe you!' Sabina laughed again, visibly relaxing. 'I wonder who this "friend" of my mother's is?' she mused curiously. Obviously having now spoken about it, she was slowly coming to terms with the fact that her mother was involved with someone.

'Why don't you ask her next time you talk to her?' he prompted lightly. 'She would probably appreciate that.'

'Maybe,' Sabina acknowledged noncommittally, not sure she actually wanted to go that far. 'Tell me, when and where do you intend holding your next exhibition?' she abruptly changed the subject, obviously having decided she had told him enough about her private life for one evening.

Well, not in Brice's eyes she hadn't; there were still dozens of things he wanted to know about Sabina Smith! Even if he did accept that some of them would have to wait…

'Richard told me that he attended the exhibition you had two years ago,' she added coolly. 'He said it was very successful.'

Brice didn't doubt that the other man had said that; he just knew that Sabina had really mentioned Richard as a reminder—just in case Brice might have forgotten—that she had a fiancé in her life…

As if he could forget with that damn great rock glittering on her left hand. But that didn't mean he wouldn't like to forget all about Richard Latham. In fact, the more he got to know Sabina, the more he wished the other man would just evaporate into thin air!

This evening wasn't going too badly, Sabina decided with inward relief. Brice McAllister was certainly easy enough to talk to. Too much so, on occasion.

'Mmm, this looks wonderful,' she enthused as her asparagus and Brice's escargot were brought to the table.

'I have no doubt that it will taste as good as it looks.' Brice nodded indulgently. 'Do you—? Oh, no…!' he groaned impatiently.

Sabina looked across at him curiously, only to find he was looking towards the doorway at a couple who had just entered the restaurant. Sabina vaguely recognised the woman as Chloe Fox, the fashion designer 'Foxy', having met her a couple of times, but she had no idea who the man was with her.

Although he looked enough like Brice, very tall, dark,

with an arrogant handsomeness, for Sabina to question the likeness.

'My cousin Fergus, and his wife Chloe,' Brice provided with obvious irritation, his displeasure with the other couple's arrival also obvious, at least, to Sabina. She hoped the other couple, having now seen Brice and walking purposefully towards their table, couldn't see it too!

Brice stood up politely. 'Fergus. Chloe,' he greeted tightly before moving to kiss Chloe lightly on the cheek. 'May I introduce Sabina?' he added with obvious reluctance.

'You certainly may. Although I'm sure we would both have recognised you without the introduction.' Fergus shook Sabina's hand warmly before turning back to this cousin. 'We're not interrupting anything, I hope?' Eyes of chocolate-brown tauntingly met Brice's frosty green ones.

Sabina found she liked the teasing affection Fergus showed towards his cousin. It made Brice McAllister seem much less arrogantly self-assured. Altogether less dangerous...

'Would the two of you care to join us?' she invited the other couple softly, keeping her expression deadpan as she saw the unmistakable look of warning irritation Brice shot in his cousin's direction.

'I'm sure you and Brice would much rather be alone,' Chloe was the one to answer her, but her dark brows were raised over speculative blue eyes as she looked across at Brice.

'Of course we wouldn't,' Sabina replied smoothly. 'It will be much more fun if there are four of us. Brice has very kindly taken pity on me while my fiancé is away on business and brought me out to dinner,' she added pointedly.

'Oh, Brice is well known for his kindness,' Fergus mocked even as he pulled back a chair for his wife to sit down before sitting down himself.

'Well known,' Brice muttered disagreeably as he resumed his own seat at the table.

'Have some wine, Fergus. Don't mind if I do, Brice,'
his cousin carried out a conversation with himself as Brice
now sat in stony silence, Fergus signalling the waiter to
bring over a couple of wineglasses so that he and Chloe
might join them in sipping the white wine.

Sabina smiled at his obvious mockery of his cousin,
becoming more sure by the second that inviting the other
couple to join them had been a good move on her part;
Brice didn't seem half as daunting in the company of his
cousin and his wife!

'Please don't let your food get cold,' Chloe advised
lightly as a waiter discreetly set two more places at the
table. 'Fergus and I can look at the menus while the two
of you eat,' she added happily.

Sabina watched Brice beneath lowered lashes as she resumed eating her asparagus; anyone looking at him as he
hooked the snails out of their shells, before grinding them
between those even white teeth, would have thought each
and every one of them had done him some personal dis-
service.

For the first time in their acquaintance Sabina had the
feeling that Brice was at something of a disadvantage. It
was a pleasant feeling!

Despite the fact that Brice added little to the conversation as the meal progressed, Sabina found she was enjoying herself. Chloe and Fergus were lively conversational-
ists, with a teasing sense of humour, and their love for
each other was in every glance they exchanged. The fact
that Brice glowered at the two of them for the next two
hours seemed to bother them not one bit.

'I believe we're going to be distantly related,' Chloe
observed much later in the evening as the four of them
lingered over coffee.

Sabina saw the sharp look of surprise Brice shot his

cousin-in-law. And she had to admit, she was a little puzzled herself. 'I'm sorry...?' she prompted frowningly.

Chloe smiled. 'My older sister is married to your fiancé's nephew,' she explained. 'I'm sure once you're married that must give us some sort of family connection—although for the life of me I can't work out what it is!' she added laughingly.

Neither could Sabina. Especially as there would never be a wedding! But what shocked her the most was that she hadn't given her 'fiancé' a thought for the last two hours. Not one...

'It does sound rather complicated,' she dismissed vaguely before turning to Brice. 'I'm sorry to break up the evening, but I believe it's time I went home.'

His mouth tightened with displeasure; obviously he hadn't liked the fact that they had shared their evening with Fergus and Chloe, but he disliked the idea of her ending the evening even more.

Which was all the more reason to end it!

She had been unwise to come out with him at all this evening, knew he was not a man she could easily spend time with. It had been pure luck—on her part—that his cousin and his wife happened to be here too.

'Maybe we'll get a chance to work together some time soon,' Chloe told Sabina warmly as she and Fergus prepared to leave, the two men in some quiet dispute over who was paying the bill.

'Maybe,' Sabina answered noncommittally, knowing her appointment book was completely full for the next six months. Thank goodness! She already knew that the less she had to do with this dynamic family, the better.

'I was so sorry we didn't get to work together last year, after all,' Chloe added softly. 'But I believe you were ill at the time?'

Sabina gave the other woman a sharp look. What—?

'Harper Manor in November,' Chloe enlarged lightly. 'I was showing a line of evening dresses that weekend.'

Sabina stared at the other woman, clearly remembering now—too late—that she had been scheduled to wear a couple of those dresses at that particular show.

'I hope it was nothing too serious?' Chloe continued concernedly.

Sabina, never particularly big on small talk anyway, found herself completely struck dumb.

This was just too much. First that letter earlier today, and now a reminder of her absence from the catwalk last November. It was just—

'What wasn't too serious?' Brice frowned at the two women, obviously having now come to some sort of agreement with his cousin concerning the bill—as he had insisted initially, he was paying it!

Chloe turned to smile at him. 'I was just reminding Sabina that the two of us should have worked together last year, but she wasn't well.'

Brice looked at Sabina with narrowed eyes. 'What was wrong with you?'

So blunt. So straightforward. So unanswerable!

'Really, Brice,' Chloe spluttered affectionately. 'You can't just demand to know about someone's illness in that way!'

'Why can't I?' He frowned. 'You mentioned Sabina was ill last year. I merely want to know what was wrong with her.' He shrugged, as if he couldn't see what the problem was.

Whereas Sabina could see what it was all too clearly! She simply didn't talk about her absence from modelling at the end of the previous year. And she had no intention of doing so now.

Chloe gave Brice a reproving look, obviously now regretting having mentioned the subject at all. 'Really, Brice, we women have to have some secrets,' she rebuked lightly.

'It was really nothing of great importance,' Sabina dismissed coolly; the last thing she wanted was for Brice to think there was something mysterious about her absence from modelling the previous year! 'Just a touch of flu,' she excused. 'It's been lovely meeting both of you,' she told the other couple sincerely—if nothing else, they had been a very welcome diversion from spending the evening alone with Brice.

Although that was probably being unfair to Chloe and Fergus; the other couple were interesting people in their own right, Chloe a fashion designer of some repute, Fergus an internationally successful author. And at any other time Sabina would have enjoyed talking to them. Just not this evening.

And not now. Now she just wanted to get away from here, back to the house where she felt safe. Away from Brice McAllister.

'Maybe we can do this again some time?' Fergus was the one to answer her smoothly.

'I doubt it—my fiancé arrives back from New York tomorrow.' Her smile was politely apologetic. 'As I told you earlier, Brice was just taking pity on me by taking me out to dinner this evening,' she added firmly.

'That wasn't true, you know,' Brice told her once they were seated in the back of the taxi on their way to the home she shared with Richard. 'What you said back there, about my taking pity on you,' he added hardly. 'Inviting you out to dinner had nothing to do with pity—I wanted to spend the evening with you.'

Sabina suddenly found the confines of the taxi claustrophobic, her breath constricting in her throat. And Brice's closeness to her on the leather seat, his trouser-clad thigh brushing lightly against hers, his arm draped casually across the seat behind her shoulders, did nothing to help alleviate the situation.

He was just too close to her. Too forcefully male. Too magnetically attractive. Just too everything!

She turned to him in the semi-darkness, feeling compelled to say something, anything. 'Brice—'

'Sabina!' he murmured raggedly before his head lowered and his mouth claimed hers.

This shouldn't be happening! She was engaged to Richard. And maybe it was only a business arrangement, an 'understanding', but she still owed him her loyalty. Her gratitude.

As Brice continued to kiss her her body was suffused with a weightless lethargy, like a soaring bird, lifted high by the heated air beneath its wings, all sound stopped, everything but Brice ceasing to exist, only the feel of Brice's lips against hers important.

She couldn't have broken away from him if she had tried.

Not that she did try, pleasure such as she had never known existed coursing through her body, every part of her electrically alive now, her arms moving up about Brice's shoulders, their bodies fused together from chest to thigh as she began to kiss him back.

'That will be eight pounds fifty, guv.'

Sabina felt as if she had had a glass of cold water thrown over her, so instant was the shocked recognition of exactly what she was doing; instead of coolly repulsing Brice McAllister's kisses she had been returning them with equal passion!

She pulled back from the close proximity of him, blue eyes huge in the semi-darkness of the taxi.

Brice stared back at her, his expression unreadable, eyes remote and unfathomable, only the tell-tale passion-induced flush to the rigid hardness of his cheeks to show for the minutes they had just spent lost in each other's arms.

'Sorry to interrupt, love.' The taxi driver turned to speak

apologetically to Sabina. 'But we've been parked outside the house for about five minutes now.'

Outside Richard's house. Her fiancé's house. The house Sabina shared with him.

She drew in a deeply controlling breath. 'That's perfectly all right,' she told the driver smoothly before turning to open the door. 'No, Brice, please don't bother to get out.' To her chagrin her voice was much less controlled as she spoke to him; she was completely unable to look at him, either.

And she might as well have spoken to the door for all the notice Brice took of her!

She had hardly straightened from getting out of the taxi than he was standing beside her, having got out the other side.

'Sabina—'

'Please don't say anything, Brice,' she interrupted much more firmly than she actually felt, her head back proudly now in the darkness as she forced herself to meet his narrowed gaze. 'I very much enjoyed meeting Fergus and Chloe this evening. And thank you for dinner,' she added with a politeness she was far from feeling.

'You don't have to tell me that it will never happen again,' he cut in harshly.

'None of this evening will ever happen again,' she told him in a steely voice. 'Goodnight.' She turned on her heel and walked away, leaving him to get back in the taxi, or not, whatever his choice might be. As long as she escaped his overwhelming presence, she didn't care what he did!

Oh, God…!

Sabina leant weakly back against the solid oak front door once she was safely on the other side of it.

What had she just done?

What had they both just done?

More to the point, how did she explain to Richard, without actually telling him the truth, and totally null-and-voiding their 'arrangement', that she could no longer sit for Brice McAllister?

CHAPTER SIX

'DINNER not to your liking, Mr Brice?' Mrs Potter frowned at him as she cleared away his almost untouched plate of food.

'Dinner was fine, Mrs Potter,' Brice rasped. 'I'm just not hungry.'

He was too damned angry to be hungry. With Sabina. With Richard Latham. With himself.

Most of all with himself.

It had been three days since his dinner with Sabina. Three long, frustrating, lonely days.

Strange, loneliness was something he had never known in his life before, not even when he'd been alone. In fact, solitude to him had always been something to be welcomed, enjoyed, savoured. But all that had changed three days ago. From the moment he'd kissed Sabina.

Something had happened to him as he'd held her in his arms, as his mouth had explored hers, as she'd kissed him back with equal passion. Something he still couldn't put a name to. Something he didn't want to put a name to. All he knew was that he now knew what loneliness was, that his own company was the last thing he wanted.

Because when he was alone all he could think about was Sabina. What was she doing? Who was she with? Had she thought of him at all the last three days?

His mouth tightened frustratedly as he acknowledged that even if Sabina had thought of him it would not have been in any sort of complimentary way. How could it be, when he had abused her trust in him by overstepping the line that should have divided them?

God, he disgusted himself, so how could he expect her to feel any differently towards him?

Sabina was engaged to another man!

Much as Brice hated it, much as he might wish it were otherwise, it was undeniably a fact. And Sabina could only despise him for choosing to forget that.

It had been a moment of pure madness on his part, a need, pure and simple, to hold her in his arms and kiss her. And now he would probably never see her again, was sure she would never agree to sit for him again.

Although the fact that Richard Latham hadn't turned up on his doorstep demanding an explanation for Brice's behaviour towards his fiancée seemed to point to her not having told the other man that Brice had kissed her…

So how was she going to explain to Richard Latham her complete aversion to even being in the same room as Brice? Maybe she wouldn't be able to. Maybe—

Hell, he had to get out of here, do something—anything! His thoughts kept going round and round in circles, always coming back to exactly the same spot: his need to see Sabina, and the knowledge that he wasn't able to.

How—?

Mrs Potter entered the room after the briefest of knocks. 'Miss Smith is here to see you, Mr Brice,' she told him warmly.

Miss Smith—? Sabina! Here to see him…?

Mrs Potter gave him a quizzical frown. 'Shall I ask her to come in?' she prompted doubtfully.

'Yes! I mean, no. Oh, hell,' he grated, running a hand through the thick darkness of his hair.

Hair that was already tousled into disarray by his agitated fingers constantly running through it all day. He hadn't shaved the last two days, either. And, he realised as he looked down at the clothes he had on, this morning he seemed to have stepped straight back into the things he had been wearing yesterday, blue denims and black shirt, and they were both badly creased. In fact, Brice decided self-disgustedly, he looked a damned mess!

But with Sabina waiting outside in the hallway, he could hardly go upstairs, shower, shave, and change before inviting her in...

'Yes, please ask her to come in,' he instructed heavily, while at the same time his mind was racing. 'Is she alone, Mrs Potter?' He frowned, wondering if Richard Latham was with her.

'Completely alone,' Sabina coolly answered that particular question herself as she joined Mrs Potter in the doorway.

She looked sensational!

If Brice looked an unkempt mess, Sabina was glossily beautiful, wearing a glittering gold dress the same colour as that long hair cascading down her back and over her shoulders, her eyes luminous blue, lips painted a voluptuous red, long fingernails painted with the same colour varnish, her legs long and silky, delicate feet slipped into three-inch-high gold sandals. To Brice, she had never looked lovelier.

'Thank you, Mrs Potter,' he told his housekeeper harshly.

'Would you like me to bring you anything? Coffee? Tea? Some wine, perhaps?' Mrs Potter offered lightly.

'That's very kind of you—' Sabina bestowed a glowing smile on the older woman '—but I won't be staying long. I only called in on my way somewhere else.'

The last, Brice was sure, was added for his benefit. Completely unnecessarily. The fact that Sabina was here at all was unexpected; he certainly didn't delude himself into thinking she had dressed like this just to come and see him!

'What do you want?' he demanded as soon as the door had closed behind the departing Mrs Potter.

Sabina eyed him coolly. 'You really are the rudest man I've ever met,' she told him calmly.

He raised dark brows mockingly. 'At least I'm consistent.'

'True,' she drawled dismissively. 'I called in—'

'You said that,' he rasped.

'Because I know Richard intends ringing you tomorrow about commissioning the portrait,' she continued firmly. 'I want you to tell him that you can't do it,' she added hardly.

Brice eyed her with mocking amusement. 'And why should I do that?'

Sabina's gaze remained unblinkingly steady on his. 'I'm sure I don't have to explain why.'

No, she didn't have to—but there was no way, after the three days of torment he had just gone through, that he could let her off the hook so easily. Besides, the mask of polite indifference that she was showing him tonight irritated him immensely!

'You're referring to the fact that we kissed each other the other evening?' he challenged.

An angry flush darkened her cheeks. 'Besides being rude, Brice, you obviously have a selective memory,' she snapped. 'You kissed me—'

'Only initially,' he drawled in a bored voice. 'I seem to remember that you kissed me back.' He raised challenging brows.

Sabina drew in an angry breath. 'You-are-not-a-gentleman!' she bit out tautly.

Oh, yes, he was—because if he followed his ungentlemanly instincts right now, he would end up kissing her again; she was absolutely magnificent in her anger!

His mouth twisted derisively. 'And I suppose Latham is?'

She stiffened, her eyes glittering coldly blue. 'Exactly what do you mean by that remark?'

Brice shrugged. 'I don't suppose for a moment that

Latham sleeps in one bedroom of that big house the two of you share, while you sleep virginally in another!' he scorned.

If he had thought her coldly distant before, she now became the ice maiden, every desirable inch of her withdrawn behind an icy barrier Brice knew he could have no hope of penetrating.

'I don't believe that is any of your business, Mr McAllister,' she spat the last out contemptuously. 'I came here this evening hoping to appeal to your better nature—but you obviously don't have one, so—'

'Latham doesn't know about the other evening, does he?' Brice took a calculated guess, more or less sure he was right, but needing to know for certain.

She flushed. 'Richard is aware that I saw you that evening—'

'That isn't what I meant—and you know it!' he rasped.

'Tell me, Brice, can you still walk?' she taunted.

He looked down at his denim-clad legs as he stood across the room from her. 'Obviously,' he drawled.

'Then I think you can take a calculated guess that I haven't told Richard of your—overfamiliarity the other evening,' she drawled mockingly.

Brice smiled without humour. 'What you really mean is that your future husband is nothing but a thug!'

All the time knowing that if Sabina were his fiancée he would feel violent himself just at the thought of any other man kissing her, let alone actually knowing he had done so!

Sabina gave him a disgusted glance. 'You—'

'How's your mother?' Brice abruptly changed the subject, sensing Sabina was about to leave, and knowing a desperate need for her not to do so.

Having her come here at all was completely unexpected; after the other evening, Brice had been certain Sabina would ensure he never saw her alone again. The fact that she had come here like this was evidence of just how much she didn't want Richard Latham to know that, not only had Brice taken her out to dinner the other evening, but that the two of them had ended the evening by kissing each other.

Evidence of how much she loved the other man...?

She looked nonplussed now by his change of topic. 'I haven't spoken to my mother since the day we had lunch together,' Sabina answered warily.

'Putting off the evil moment?' Brice chided softly. 'Is that being completely fair to your mother? After all, from the little you told me, I doubt you were very gracious that day about her proposed holiday plans.'

Her cheeks became flushed once again. 'I really don't think this is any of your business, Brice—'

'Coward,' he murmured softly.

Her eyes widened indignantly. 'Not that it's anything to do with you—but I have every intention of talking to my mother. In my own way. In my own time.'

He nodded grimly. 'And, in the meantime, she can just sit there and stew in her own juice!'

Sabina frowned. 'You know nothing about my mother—'

'I know she cared enough to take the time and trouble to come to London to tell you about her proposed holiday to Paris, with a male friend,' Brice rasped. 'Even though she probably knew exactly how you were going to react,' he added tauntingly.

Sabina was all eyes now, huge blue pools of pained disbelief. Because he was deliberately attacking her, challenging her. But he couldn't help that; the cool Sabina, behind her wall of ice, was not acceptable to him.

Because from the moment she had arrived what he had most wanted to do was kiss her again!

Sabina swallowed hard, giving Brice a quizzical look. He looked different today, and it wasn't just the several days' growth of beard that darkened his jaw, or his rumpled hair and clothes. Those things could easily be explained in an artist of his calibre who became lost in whatever he was working on at the moment.

No, it was something else... She just didn't know what it was!

'And exactly how was that?' she finally breathed huskily.

He shrugged. 'It's okay for you to live with a man old enough to be your father, but heaven help your mother if she tries to find a little happiness of her own in her twilight years,' he rasped scathingly.

She shook her head, smiling without humour, unappreciative of any of his remark, but especially the part about Richard being old enough to be her father. 'I doubt my mother considers she has reached that at only sixty-six!' Her mother came from a long line of octogenarians.

'Exactly,' Brice pounced pointedly. 'Hell, if it were me, I would say good luck to her!'

There were plenty of replies she could have made to such a remark; predominantly that, from the safety of his own parents' obvious longevity of married life, he was hardly in a position to say how he would feel in the same circumstances.

But Sabina had finally realised exactly what Brice was doing—and she wasn't going to give him the satisfaction of being successful. Because, like a small boy, he was trying to pick a fight...

She shook her head. 'I didn't come here to discuss my mother with you, Brice.'

His mouth twisted. 'No—you came here to ask me to tell your fiancé—when he telephones!—that I can't paint you.'

And she could tell, just from looking at his face, that he wasn't going to do that!

'I've obviously wasted my time,' she acknowledged with a sigh before glancing at the slender gold watch on her wrist. 'I really don't have any more time to discuss this with you now, Brice—'

'You mustn't keep Richard waiting,' he taunted hardly. 'And I expect the attentive Clive is sitting outside in the car waiting for you too,' he added scathingly.

'Richard isn't with me this evening,' she dismissed impatiently. 'I'm working.'

She was attending a charity dinner with several other models this evening; Richard away on business again until tomorrow. But Brice was quite right about Clive waiting outside for her in the car. As he would also be waiting to take her home again once the evening was over...

She picked up her evening bag. 'I'm sorry we can't come to some sort of amicable agreement concerning the portrait, Brice,' she told him coolly. 'I really was hoping we could keep this on a friendly level.'

His eyes narrowed to green slits. 'Meaning?'

She shrugged slender shoulders. 'I'm not sure yet,' she answered slowly.

Brice watched her consideringly. 'And I'm not sure I like the sound of that.'

Sabina gave a brief smile. 'But I'm completely sure I don't give a damn how you feel about it!' she told him mildly before turning to leave.

'There's something I would like to know, Sabina.' Brice spoke softly behind her.

Too close behind her, it seemed to Sabina, the warmth of his breath brushing against the bareness of her shoulders.

Reminding her all too vividly of those minutes spent in his arms three days ago.

Remind her? She hadn't been able to put them out of her mind for a moment!

Oh, she had dated several men before meeting Richard

almost a year ago. And they had been pleasant friendships. But none of those relationships had been in the least serious, certainly none of those men causing her pulse to race and her body to turn to liquid fire. And now that she was engaged to Richard—for whatever reason!—was not the time to find herself reacting in that way three days ago, with Brice McAllister, of all people!

But she knew that she had…

She didn't turn to face Brice now, drawing in a steadying breath. 'And what's that, Brice?' she prompted mockingly.

'I'm curious to know what was in that letter you received in the post the other day to have caused you so much obvious distress at the time,'' he probed relentlessly. 'I'm referring to the letter in the green envelope,' he clarified unnecessarily.

Unnecessarily to Sabina, at least. She had known, as soon as he'd mentioned it, exactly which letter he was referring to!

She had become frozen, as if turned to stone, every muscle and sinew in her body locked in place, her breathing seeming to have become caught in her throat, literally able to feel all the blood draining from her face.

'Sabina…?' Brice's hand on her arm gently turned her to face him. 'Sabina!' he groaned worriedly as he saw her obvious physical reaction to his question.

She swallowed hard, trying to speak, but her tongue seemed to be stuck to the roof of her mouth. Her vision was blurring too, Brice's face no longer clear to her. And although she could see Brice's mouth moving, knew he must be saying something to her, the rushing noise in her ears prevented her from hearing him.

And then all she knew was blackness…

CHAPTER SEVEN

SHE looked so damned young with her eyes closed, Brice realised frowningly as he looked down at Sabina, the wariness in those deep blue eyes, that could give her such a look of maturity, hidden now behind closed lids, the thick dark lashes that lay against the delicate magnolia of her cheeks making her appear as vulnerable as a baby.

Brice had managed to catch her before she sank to the carpeted floor, swinging her up into his arms before placing her carefully on the sofa, her hair splayed out on the cushion behind her. Despite what she claimed to the contrary, she was as light as thistledown, and as Brice continued to look down at her, the slenderness of her body, the deep hollows of her cheeks and throat, he was sure she had lost weight in the last few days.

Because of him? Because he had kissed her?

Or was it because of that letter he had just taunted her about?

In view of her reaction just now to his asking her about it, the latter was probably a more accurate guess!

But who could it have been from? What could that letter possibly have contained to have this effect on her, days later?

He could try asking her that, Brice realised grimly, but he very much doubted Sabina would answer!

He frowned down at her as she began to stir, lids blinking open, only to close again as she saw him sitting beside her, looking intently down at her.

'Come on,' Brice mocked. 'It isn't that bad!'

She gave a grimace, as if to say, That's only from where you're looking, before slowly opening her eyes again. She swallowed hard, moistening dry lips. 'Do you think I could have a glass of water?' Her voice was huskily soft, her gaze avoiding meeting his.

'Don't move while I'm gone,' he warned even as he stood up to go out to the kitchen.

As he might have known, Sabina was sitting up on the sofa smoothing down her tousled hair by the time he returned with the water. 'Do you ever do as you're told?' he rasped, watching as she took one sip of the water before putting the glass down on the coffee-table in front of her.

'Rarely,' she grimaced. 'I'm sorry about that. I can't imagine what happened—'

'I can,' Brice said harshly. 'You don't look as if you've eaten a decent meal for days!' And he could tell by the way the colour darkened her cheeks that his guess about that was right. 'Why haven't you been eating?' he demanded to know.

Sabina looked up at him challengingly. 'I don't think my eating habits are any of your concern—'

'You just fainted in my house—so I'm making them my concern!' he bit out grimly. 'Well?' he barked as she made no effort to answer him.

She shook her head, once again glancing at her wrist-watch. 'I really do have to go—'

'I went outside after you fainted and told Clive to cancel your engagement for this evening,' Brice told her softly.

'You did what?' Sabina gasped, her eyes widening disbelievingly.

'I'm sure you heard what I said,' he drawled. 'I also told him you wouldn't be needing him any more this evening.'

Sabina opened her mouth to speak, and then closed it again. Before opening it again. And then closing it yet again.

If the situation weren't so damned serious, Brice would have found her reaction to his arrogance amusing. A speechless Sabina was certainly something to behold. And maybe he had been rather heavy-handed in his behaviour, but if Sabina wasn't prepared to look after herself, then someone else would have to do it for her. But considering Latham was such a watchdog in other ways—

'Where's Richard this evening?' he rasped.

'Away,' she managed to choke out, obviously still stunned by the way he had taken over her evening for her.

'Again?' Brice muttered disgustedly. 'And what does he think you are—a prize exhibit to be taken out and admired whenever he deigns to be at home?' He remembered all too clearly David Latham's opinion of his uncle.

Sabina looked deeply irritated. 'You're being ridiculous. Richard is a very busy man—'

'So am I,' Brice cut in scathingly. 'But I certainly wouldn't leave you on your own to get into this state.'

She glared at him resentfully. 'What state?'

Oh, she looked hauntingly beautiful, there was no doubting that. But she was so thin she looked as if he might snap her in half, and her eyes were like huge dark pools, the hollows of her cheeks only emphasising the shadows beneath those eyes.

Brice shook his head disgustedly. 'You're as skittish as an overbred racehorse—'

'Thank you very much!' she scorned.

'It wasn't meant as a compliment,' he snapped.

'I didn't take it as one,' she snapped right back.

'You—'

'Dinner is served, Mr Brice,' Mrs Potter appeared in the doorway to announce, obviously having knocked but not having been heard.

Not surprising really—when Brice and Sabina were as good as shouting at each other!

Sabina became very still. 'Dinner, Brice?' she questioned softly.

Brice wasn't deceived for a moment by the mildness of

her tone—Sabina was already furious over his having so arrogantly cancelled her plans for the evening; having the nerve to instruct Mrs Potter to serve dinner to them both here as an alternative was obviously going too far as far as she was concerned!

'We both need to eat, Sabina,' he told her dismissively; for some reason his own appetite seemed to have returned to him!

Her eyes flashed her anger at him, but the quick glance she gave in Mrs Potter's direction showed she was too ladylike to actually say to him what she really wanted to in front of his housekeeper.

Thank goodness!

Brice was well aware that his earlier actions had been arrogant in the extreme, but at the time he had been so worried about Sabina that worry had materialised as anger as she'd remained in the faint, so much so that he had marched straight out of the house and rapped out his instruction to Richard Latham's driver-watchdog, not even waiting to see if they were carried out before slamming back into the house.

He had merely compounded that arrogance by asking Mrs Potter, when he'd gone to the kitchen for the glass of water, if she could provide dinner for the two of them!

Brice turned to his housekeeper. 'We'll be through in a few minutes, Mrs Potter,' he assured her dismissively.

'How dare you?' Sabina turned on him as soon as they were alone again, standing up abruptly to glare across at him accusingly. 'How dare you?' she repeated in incredulous anger.

He shrugged. 'I think you need to eat, Sabina—'

'I'm not just talking about dinner, Brice,' she came back heatedly. 'How dare you cancel my plans for the evening? How dare you send Clive away? One kiss doesn't give you those sort of rights, Brice,' she told him scornfully.

After days of tension, Brice could feel himself starting

to relax. Because, despite her denials, he now knew that kiss had meant something to her—she wouldn't have mentioned it otherwise!

Too late for Sabina, he could see that she had just realised that for herself...

He grinned at her unabashedly. 'Ah, Sabina, but what a kiss!'

'You—I—you are incorrigible!' she finally spluttered weakly.

Brice shrugged. 'Part of my charm.'

Sabina eyed him scathingly, but with none of her earlier anger. 'Arrogance is not a virtue, Brice,' she told him derisively.

'Neither is starvation,' he dismissed lightly. 'Shall we go through to dinner?' he invited, dark brows raised challengingly as he held out his arm for her to take.

Sabina returned his gaze frustratedly, obviously fighting some sort of war within herself.

Brice waited for her to come to her decision. Not patiently. But he did wait. He had probably done enough bullying for one evening!

'Okay,' she finally sighed. 'But only as my driver has been dismissed, and my dinner this evening seems to have been cancelled,' she reminded pointedly. 'And under one condition...' she added huskily, her gaze steady on his.

Brice tensed warily. 'Which is?'

She drew in a ragged breath. 'No more questions about my personal correspondence,' she stated evenly.

Brice had thought it might be something like that, and it wasn't a condition he particularly wanted to agree to, especially after her reaction to his questions earlier. But if it meant Sabina stayed and had dinner with him without any more argument...

'Okay,' he agreed, once again filing that piece of information away for a future conversation. Because he had every intention, at some time in the not too distant future, of finding out exactly what had been in that letter.

Sabina made a point of not taking the arm he held out to her as they walked through to the dining-room. But that didn't bother Brice too much, either; now that she had agreed to have dinner with him he had her company for at least another couple of hours, so why push his luck? In any direction!

Brice might think he had won this round, Sabina realised as he saw her seated at the dining table before sitting down opposite her, but she could have told him differently. It merely took less effort to agree to have dinner with him than the alternative of having to call a taxi, sit and wait for it to arrive, and then finding something to eat when she got home.

At least...that was what she told herself.

She was actually very aware now that she had forgotten to eat at all today, feeling slightly shaky and light-headed. As if to prove the point, her stomach gave a hungry growl as Mrs Potter placed a bowl of thick vegetable soup in front of her seconds later.

Sabina looked up and smiled gratefully at the house-keeper. 'I hope I'm not inconveniencing you too much?'

'Not in the least,' the other woman assured her. 'It will be nice to see Mr Brice eat his dinner; he's been completely off his food this last few days,' she reproved her employer lightly before going back to the kitchen.

Sabina made a great show of eating her soup, unable to look at Brice for the moment, having trouble keeping her face straight; she wasn't the only one who hadn't been eating properly just recently.

'Okay, okay,' Brice muttered after several silent minutes had passed, 'so I haven't done justice to Mrs Potter's cooking the last three days, either.' He grimaced self-derisively.

Sabina sobered slightly, not sure that she liked the implication of that statement. It had been three days since she'd last had dinner with Brice. Since he had kissed her...

She had tried not to dwell on thoughts of that kiss the last three days, knowing she shouldn't think of it at all, but finding the memory of it popping back into her head when she least expected—or wanted—it to do so. Which was all the time!

'What a pity—this soup is delicious,' Sabina remarked blandly, unwilling to get into any more discussion about what had happened between them three days ago.

She was engaged to Richard, owed him so much, and the kiss between Brice and herself should never had happened. And the sooner it was forgotten, by both of them, the better she would like it!

'I've been thinking—'

'I really would like you—'

They both broke off, having started talking at the same time.

'You first,' Sabina invited.

'No, you go first,' Brice insisted. 'Despite what you may think to the contrary, I haven't forgotten my manners completely,' he added ruefully.

She shrugged. 'I was merely going to ask if you would reconsider not doing the portrait.' She paused in eating her soup to look at him expectantly.

'No,' he answered uncompromisingly.

Well, that was pretty blunt and to the point! But Brice was being altogether silly about this, must know that it wasn't a good idea for them to spend time alone together.

As they were doing now!

They made a very strange couple too, she realised ruefully; she was dressed to go out for the evening and meet the general public, and Brice, besides being unshaven, looked as if he might have slept in the clothes he was wearing.

'Sorry about this.' He seemed to become aware of at

least some of her thoughts, running a rueful hand over the stubble on his chin. 'I can go up and shave once we've finished our soup, if you would prefer it?' He raised dark brows questioningly.

She actually would have preferred it. But not for the reason he seemed to think. The truth was, Brice looked more piratical than ever with the dark growth of beard on the squareness of his jaw. Altogether too rakishly attractive.

What disconcerted her the most, though, was that Brice once again seemed to have picked up on at least some of her thoughts. Although not all of them, thank goodness!

'Please don't bother on my account, Brice. It's of absolutely no interest to me whether or not you've shaved today,' she told him coolly, aware by the tightening of his mouth that he didn't particularly care for her condescending tone.

'It seems I don't have the monopoly on rudeness,' he rasped harshly.

She sat back, her soup finished, a façade of unconcern firmly in place. 'You haven't told me yet what you were going to say earlier,' she reminded lightly.

Brice's irritated scowl looked as if he would have liked to continue the conversation they were having now, and then he shrugged it off impatiently. 'I'm going up to Scotland for a couple of days next weekend,' he rasped. 'I want you to come with me.'

Sabina stared at him disbelievingly; he couldn't really have just invited her to go to Scotland with him. Could he…?

His mouth twisted derisively as he took in her stunned expression. 'I wasn't suggesting an illicit couple of days away together,' he drawled mockingly. 'I'm going to my grandfather's castle.'

This explanation didn't make the invitation sound any

more innocent to Sabina; after all, he hadn't said his grandfather would actually be at the castle…!

'Exactly what are you suggesting, Brice?' she derided
mockingly.

'I—' He broke off as Mrs Potter returned to take away
their used soup bowls, waiting until the housekeeper had
once again departed before continuing. 'I know exactly
how and where I want to paint you,' he told her with
satisfaction.

'How and where…?' she repeated warily, not liking the
sound of this at all.

'I am not a portrait painter, Sabina,' he dismissed impatiently. 'I told your fiancé that from the beginning,' he
added frowningly.

'But you just insisted you're going to paint me,' she
reminded with a puzzled frown.

'I am going to paint you,' he confirmed enthusiastically.
'The way that you look, it would be a tragedy not to. But
I'm not intending to do some posed portrait of you; if
Latham wants that he can stick a photograph of you up on
the wall,' he added disgustedly. 'No, I want to paint you
in one of the turret rooms of my grandfather's castle, sitting at the open window, with that silken golden hair trail-
ing in the wind—'

'Wearing a diaphanous gown, and little else,' Sabina
concluded derisively. 'The name Rapunzel somehow
comes to mind!' she added tauntingly.

Although that wasn't how she was feeling inside, a nervous fluttering having begun in her stomach just at the
thought of posing for Brice looking like that. What he was
proposing was pure fantasy—and she already knew that,
where Brice McAllister was concerned, she had to keep
their relationship strictly on a feet-on-the-ground basis!

Because, if she didn't, she was very much afraid she
might get caught up in the fantasy!

CHAPTER EIGHT

BRICE could already see the refusal forming on Sabina's lips. And that was something he couldn't allow.

He didn't know how, or when, the idea had first come to him, but he had suddenly known a few minutes ago exactly how he wanted to paint Sabina. That it was the only way he could paint her!

Sabina had been staring at him wordlessly, but now she shook her head. 'I really don't think that was quite what Richard had in mind when he suggested you paint me,' she began mockingly.

'As I recall, he didn't suggest it at all,' Brice rasped impatiently, remembering only too well the other man's arrogant assumption that Brice couldn't possibly turn him down. 'And I really don't give a damn what Latham "had in mind",' he dismissed scathingly. 'If he doesn't like the painting when it's finished, I'll keep the damned thing myself!' he added firmly.

He would probably want to do that anyway, if the painting turned out to be as good as he hoped it would!

Sabina shook her head slowly. 'I really can't come to Scotland with you, Brice—'

'Why the hell not?' he demanded impatiently, fuelled with enthusiasm now that the inspiration had come to him, wanting to get started on the painting as quickly as possible. 'My grandfather will be there, so your virtue will be completely safe,' he assured her dryly.

She blinked. 'Your grandfather will be there?' she repeated doubtfully.

Brice grinned. 'Once I tell him I'm bringing the beautiful model Sabina with me, I'm sure he will,' he confirmed ruefully. 'Grandfather may be in his early eighties, but he still has an eye for a beautiful woman!'

Sabina gave a vague smile at this description of his grandfather, but otherwise continued to look unconvinced.

'Whereabouts in Scotland does your mother live?' Brice tried a different approach, knowing he had to get Sabina's agreement to his idea of the two of them going to Scotland. He just had to!

'My mother?' she repeated dazedly.

'Do try to stay up with the conversation, Sabina,' Brice taunted teasingly. 'I'm suggesting we go to Scotland. Your mother lives in Scotland too.' He deliberately spoke slowly and clearly. 'If it's anywhere near my grandfather's home you could visit her while we're there.'

Sabina shook her head, this conversation obviously running on too swiftly for her liking.

But Brice was always like this when the inspiration hit him. And, despite doing numerous sketches of her, he had been in a complete fog where painting Sabina was concerned; but he could see her at his grandfather's castle now, knew exactly how right she was going to look.

'But I've never—' Sabina broke off what she had been about to say, biting her lip distractedly.

'Never what?' Brice frowned at her. 'Never visited your mother in Scotland?' he realised incredulously. 'How long did you say she's lived there?'

'Five years,' Sabina admitted reluctantly.

'Then it's way past time you did visit her,' Brice told her disgustedly.

Her cheeks flushed resentfully at his obvious rebuke. 'I think any future plans I make to see my mother are—'

'Your concern,' Brice finished derisively. 'Probably they are. But as we're going to be in Scotland, anyway—'

'I haven't agreed to go with you yet,' Sabina protested.

'You'll need to see Chloe early next week too,' he continued frowningly. 'She—'

'Chloe?' Sabina echoed dazedly. 'You mean Chloe Fox?'

'Or Chloe McCloud, whichever you prefer.' He nodded. 'I want her to design and make a dress for you. I know exactly what it has to look like, so Chloe can actually draw the design before seeing you, and then it will just be a case of making it up to your measurements. Am I going too fast for you, Sabina?' he drawled mockingly as she was looking more and more weighed down by the minute with this bombardment of information.

'Too fast!' Sabina repeated agitatedly. 'You—' She broke off as Mrs Potter arrived to serve their main course.

More of the roast chicken that Brice hadn't been able to eat earlier, served with fresh Rosti potatoes and a mixed salad.

'It looks delicious,' Sabina told the housekeeper warmly.

'Thank you, Mrs Potter.' Brice smiled his appreciation at his housekeeper before she left the room. 'You were saying?' he prompted Sabina, even as he put a large serving of the potatoes onto her plate beside the slices of chicken.

'I have no idea how my schedule stands for next week,' she told him determinedly. 'But I very much doubt I have a couple of days free in which to go up to Scotland. Even if I wanted to go,' she added irritably.

'Which you don't,' Brice easily guessed.

'Which I don't,' she echoed forcefully.

'Hmm,' he murmured consideringly. 'You work too hard, you know. Why is that?' he mused lightly. 'You've been at the top for years now, so it certainly can't be because of the money—or can it?' He stopped frowningly.

That letter she had received in the distinctive green envelope; was it possible that someone was blackmailing her? Over what, Brice couldn't even begin to imagine, but it would certainly provide an answer to more than a few questions that had been bothering Brice since the day she had received that letter…!

'Sabina—'

'It isn't the money, Brice,' she told him with certainty. 'I—like to work, to keep busy.' She gave an overbright smile. 'After all, models have a very short shelf-life; I can't expect to be at the top for much longer.'

As an attempt at diverting the conversation, it wasn't bad, Brice conceded. If he were the type of man that was easily diverted. Which he wasn't.

'Good try, Sabina,' he drawled. 'Now what's the real reason?'

Her eyes flashed deeply blue. 'I've just told you,' she snapped. 'Just as I've told you I can't disappear up to Scotland next week on such short notice,' she added impatiently. 'I have work. Commitments.'

Latham, Brice realised. No doubt the other man wouldn't be too happy at the idea of Sabina going off with him for a few days, even if it was so that Brice could paint her. The only way around that Brice could see was to include the other man in the invitation. Which was something Brice was very loath to do…

He wanted Sabina to himself, he realised, even if it were only for two days. He wanted to get to know her, away from London, her work commitments, Latham. Most of all, away from Latham!

He grimaced. 'Perhaps if I explain the situation to your fiancé—'

'Richard will be away in Australia all next week—' Sabina broke off her protest as she realised what she had just said. 'I'm due to join him at the weekend,' she added defensively.

Brice was well aware of the reason for that defence— he had been unable to hide his elation at the news that Richard Latham would be out of the country next week!

'What a pity he won't be able to join us,' Brice said

insincerely. 'But surely there can't be too much of a problem if you delay joining him until Monday,' he reasoned
with satisfaction.

Yes! Things couldn't have worked out better if he had
planned the whole thing himself!

Sabina gave a sigh. 'You're very persistent, Brice,' she
said heavily.

And, with her admission that Latham wouldn't even be
in the country next week, she had left herself with no fea-
sible argument against Brice's plan. Except the fact that
she obviously didn't want to go to Scotland with him...

Why didn't she?

She had come here at all this evening for the sole reason
of persuading Brice into telling Richard Latham he
couldn't paint her portrait. Why? Had the kiss they had
shared three days ago affected her more than she cared to
admit?

If so, as far as Brice was concerned, there was even
more reason for them to go to Scotland together. Sabina
might be engaged to Richard Latham, but she couldn't
possibly go ahead and marry the other man if she was
attracted to *him*!

Sabina had little appetite for the food in front of her, too
churned up by the fact that she had talked herself into a
corner where Brice's idea of going to Scotland was concerned. The trouble was, Brice tied her up in knots, so that
what she really meant to say came out all wrong.

She had come here this evening with the sole intention
of never seeing Brice again—and instead she found herself
with a potential weekend with him in Scotland!

It just wasn't possible.

'I'm sorry, Brice, but I really do have to go now.' She
placed her knife and fork on the plate beside the almost
untouched food.

'Why?'

She wasn't fooled for a minute by the mildness of his tone, knew by those narrowed green eyes that his mood was far from mild. 'Because I want to,' she told him firmly, pushing back her chair to stand up.

He grimaced, standing up too. 'Mrs Potter will probably hand her notice in after this; it's the second time this evening that the dinner she prepared has gone uneaten!'

Sabina gave a rueful smile. 'I'm sure you're more than capable of handling Mrs Potter's disappointment.' In fact, she was sure that Brice was more than capable of handling most situations!

But she wasn't. And her nerve-endings had taken enough of a battering for one evening. 'Could I use your telephone to call a taxi?' she prompted huskily. As Brice had arbitrarily cancelled all her other plans for this evening, the thought of a long soak in the bath, and then a good night's sleep, was very inviting.

'I'll drive you home—'

''No,' Sabina cut in with quiet firmness. 'I think you've already done enough for me for one evening!'

Her sarcasm wasn't lost on Brice, his mouth tightening angrily at the jibe. Well, she couldn't help that; there was no getting away from the fact that he had cancelled her other plans for this evening. Or that she needed to get away from Brice, not spend more time in the confines of a car with him!

'Fine,' he finally rasped. 'I'll go and call a taxi for you now.' He strode forcefully out of the room.

That wasn't quite what she had said, but by this time Sabina felt too weary to argue with him any further. Besides, the few minutes' respite from Brice's overpowering company gave her a chance to try and ease the tension from her body.

What was it about Brice McAllister that made it so difficult for her to be in his company? Somehow she didn't think she really wanted an answer to that question. In fact, she was sure she didn't!

'The taxi will be here in a few minutes,' Brice informed her abruptly when he came back into the room. 'I'm completely serious about the two of us going to Scotland next weekend, Sabina,' he added firmly.

She knew he was serious—she just didn't want to do it. And if she didn't want to do it, she saw no reason why she should!

'We'll see,' she answered noncommittally; much as she hated to admit it, she knew she would be able to deal much more capably with this situation once she was well away from Brice.

'We most certainly will,' Brice returned determinedly.

The few minutes waiting for the taxi were not the most comfortable Sabina had ever spent, their conversation stilted to say the least, both of them heaving a sigh of relief, Sabina was sure, when the taxi finally arrived.

To her consternation Brice walked outside with her, opening the back door of the taxi for her. Sabina hesitated before getting inside, not quite sure what to say. She couldn't exactly thank him for a pleasant evening—it had been far from that!—but she somehow felt she should say something.

'You don't have to say anything,' Brice advised dryly as he seemed to read her uncertainty. 'A kiss will suffice,' he added softly even as his head lowered and his mouth claimed hers.

Sabina was initially too surprised to resist. And then as the kiss deepened and lengthened she found that she couldn't have moved away even if she had wanted to— her body simply felt too fluid to obey her commands!

Brice moved slightly away from her, one hand cupping the curve of her chin as he looked down intently into her eyes. 'I'll call you,' he told her huskily.

Sabina moved hastily away, her cheeks heated as she

got inside the taxi and closed the door firmly behind her before giving the driver her address, angry with herself as well as with Brice.

She kept her gaze firmly ahead as the car moved away from the pavement, although she was completely aware of Brice standing there watching her until the car turned the corner at the end of the road.

How dared he just kiss her whenever, and wherever, he felt like it? Almost as if he were her fiancé instead of Richard—

Dear Lord—Richard!

What on earth would he say if he knew that Brice McAllister had kissed her, not once, but twice?

She gave a self-disgusted shake of her head. Richard respected the fact that they both had busy careers, that the business relationship of their engagement worked because Richard knew he could trust her, as she trusted him. Okay, so she hadn't initiated either of the kisses between Brice and herself, but she hadn't exactly tried to stop them, either.

Why hadn't she?

That was something she really didn't want to look at too searchingly! Once she could perhaps explain away, but that kiss just now had been completely unacceptable. Not that she had initiated it, but nevertheless it shouldn't have happened.

But she didn't ever intend telling Richard about those kisses. Their own relationship wasn't an intimate one, and it would only create a situation where she was determined there should be none.

To her surprise most of the lights were on downstairs in the house when she arrived home, her relief immense when she entered the house to find Richard in the lounge listening to classical music. Something he seemed to have been doing for some time, if the glass of whisky on the table beside him was anything to go by.

'I wasn't expecting you back until tomorrow.' She smiled at him warmly.

Richard had stood up at her entry, his eyes narrowed now as he looked at her speculatively. 'Obviously not,' he drawled hardly.

Sabina was instantly—guiltily!—aware of the fact that not fifteen minutes ago Brice McAllister had kissed her. Did it somehow show on her face? Were her lips bare of gloss after that kiss? Or was it something else that gave her away...?

Richard turned to pick up his glass of whisky, taking a swallow before speaking. 'Clive returned over an hour ago,' he rasped economically, blond brows raised questioningly.

A Clive who had been arrogantly dismissed for the evening by Brice McAllister...!

She winced at the construction Richard must have put on being told that by the driver. 'I called in to see Brice McAllister on my way out this evening—'

'Yes?' Richard prompted hardly as she paused.

She sighed. 'Could I have a small glass of whisky too, do you think?'

Richard's mouth twisted derisively, even as he moved to pour the drink for her. 'Is what you're going to tell me that bad?' he prompted as he handed her the glass.

Sabina gave him a sharp look, the whisky having warmed her on its way down. 'I don't understand...?'

He shrugged, moving away slightly. 'We've both known from the beginning that our engagement is purely a business arrangement, and you've obviously just spent the evening with McAllister—'

'Hardly the evening, Richard,' she interrupted lightly. 'It's only nine-thirty now. Actually, I called in to see Brice this evening to—to—to—'

'To what, Sabina?' Richard prompted softly.

'To arrange another sitting,' she burst out in what she

knew was a defensive tone. But she couldn't help it; she simply wasn't prepared for answering Richard's probing questions so soon after Brice had kissed her. Because she felt guilty even though she hadn't been the one to initiate that kiss!

'Why not just telephone him?'

Why not, indeed? 'I was passing, anyway.' She shrugged.

'And?' Richard frowned.

'Richard, you're home a day early; let's not waste the evening talking about Brice McAllister,' she dismissed lightly, hugging his arm as she sensed his tension.

'But I don't consider it a waste of the evening,' he came back softly. 'Have you spent other evenings at McAllister's while I've been away?' he prompted lightly.

'Certainly not.' She shook her head frowningly. 'Richard, it was nothing. I didn't want to tell you this—I know how you worry—but I went to Brice McAllister's to arrange a sitting, and I—well, the truth is, I fainted,' she admitted reluctantly.

'You fainted?' he repeated frowningly, grasping her arms to look down at her searchingly. 'What's happened, Sabina? You haven't received any more of those letters?' He scowled darkly.

'No, nothing like that,' she instantly assured him. Although it had been Brice's probing about those letters that had caused her to faint. 'I forgot to eat today, that's all,' she explained with a self-conscious grimace.

'That's all?' Richard echoed reprovingly. 'You silly girl,' he rebuked huskily. 'And I've been sitting here for the last hour with all manner of thoughts going through my mind,' he admitted self-derisively. 'Have you had something to eat now?' he prompted gently.

She nodded. 'Brice insisted on feeding me.' No need to tell Richard that, because of the subject of their conversation, she hadn't been able to eat anything but a bowl of soup!

She had known from the beginning that Richard was possessive, but that possessiveness also made him protective of what he considered his. And these last few months, that was exactly what she had needed...

'Good.' Richard gave her a warm smile. 'I'm sorry if I was less than welcoming a few minutes ago. It's just that you're so beautiful, so absolutely unique—' He shook his head ruefully. 'I should have known better than to doubt you.'

Sabina swallowed hard, knowing that he wasn't altogether wrong to doubt her...

CHAPTER NINE

'WHAT do you mean, you want to bring some girl up here?' his grandfather's voice sounded impatient down the telephone line.

'Exactly that, Grandfather,' Brice replied frowningly.

He had thought it only right, before pursuing the matter with either Sabina or Richard Latham, to ask his grandfather if he minded him bringing a guest with him to Scotland next weekend. He certainly hadn't expected this reaction to his request!

'This isn't a hotel, laddie.' His grandfather's brogue deepened in his agitation. 'I know you boys have never thought so, but I do have a life of my own to live,' he added truculently. 'I don't just sit around here waiting for one of you to honour me with one of your random visits!'

Oops—he really had caught his grandfather on a bad day! And Brice was well aware of how busy the estate in Scotland kept his grandfather, the castle accompanied by several thousand acres of land, some of it given over to the breeding of deer, but the rest of it divided up amongst numerous tenants who lived on the estate. Which, despite the presence of an estate manager, still kept his grandfather very busy.

It was also quite amusing the way his grandfather still referred to Logan, Fergus, and Brice as 'boys'; they were all thirty-six years old, which hardly made them boys!

'Besides,' his grandfather continued before Brice could answer him, 'it's just possible I may have a guest of my own staying next weekend.'

'A guest, Grandfather?' Brice echoed interestedly.

'I do have friends of my own, laddie,' his grandfather rasped.

'Would this guest we're talking about happen to be female?' Brice guessed curiously.

Strange as Brice might find the idea, his grandfather was still a handsome man even though in his early eighties, and he had also been a widower for some years now...

'Don't get cheeky with me, laddie,' his grandfather snapped.

'We are talking about a female guest,' Brice realised slightly incredulously. It was one thing to make the suggestion, another to have it confirmed...!

'We aren't talking about her at all,' his grandfather bit out decisively.

'You aren't the "kiss and tell" type, are you, Grandfather?' Brice drawled mockingly, not altogether sure he was comfortable with the reversal of roles.

'Watch your tongue, boy,' the elderly man came back harshly.

This was a complication Brice had just never envisaged, he had to admit. And he wasn't a hundred per cent sure he knew how to deal with it now that it had happened!

So much for his advice to Sabina to be adult where her mother's relationship was concerned—this was his grandfather, not one of his parents, and he didn't know how to handle it!

'So the answer is no, Grandfather?' he said slowly.

'Now, I didn't say that,' the older man came back dismissively. 'I'm merely trying to point out that my home is not a hotel, somewhere for you to bring the current woman in your life—'

'Sabina isn't the current woman in my life.' More's the pity, Brice could have added regretfully. 'I've accepted a commission to paint her, that's all.' That was all!

His peace of mind had been in turmoil since the other

week when he'd first seen Sabina! And he wasn't sure that painting her was going to get her out of his system, either.

'Sabina?' his grandfather echoed sharply. 'You aren't talking about the model Sabina?'

'The one and only,' Brice confirmed wryly. 'Although I didn't know you kept up with the fashion world, Grandfather,' he added derisively. Although it wouldn't be all that difficult to have seen photographs of Sabina; her face had been adorning the front page of magazines for five years or so now.

'You don't know everything about me, Brice,' the older man scorned.

'Obviously not,' Brice confirmed dryly; he had certainly never heard anything about his grandfather having a woman staying with him before. And he didn't think Logan or Fergus had, either, otherwise they would have been sure to mention it.

'When are you thinking of coming up?' his grandfather prompted thoughtfully.

'I'm not sure. I wanted to confirm it was okay with you before making any definite plans.' And, from the sound of it, it was just as well that he had!

'It's fine with me,' his grandfather assured him lightly.

Brice frowned slightly. His grandfather hadn't sounded as if it were fine with him a few minutes ago...

'Then I'll call you later in the week to confirm a time, if that's okay with you?' he said slowly.

He had an appointment to see Richard Latham in just over an hour's time, would know better then whether or not he was going to be able to take Sabina to Scotland with him. He would have much rather just dealt with Sabina herself, but as Richard Latham was the one commissioning the painting, and—unfortunately!—he was also Sabina's fiancé, Brice had accepted it was Latham he would have to talk to.

Although he was hoping that Sabina would be there too…

It had been two days since she'd left his home so abruptly, two long days when Brice had thought of little else. But he had deliberately left it a couple of days before arranging to meet with Richard Latham; for one, he wanted to give Sabina time to get over being angry with him, for two, he hadn't wanted to look too eager!

Mostly, he admitted self-derisively, it was the latter.

All of his waking moments now, it seemed, were spent in thinking about Sabina, in remembering how she felt in his arms, the taste and feel of her lips against his.

He could never remember being this obsessed with a woman in his life before. A woman who was completely unattainable!

'Fine,' his grandfather answered him. 'But do be sure to let me know what time you're arriving,' he added warningly.

'I'll try not to catch you at an embarrassing moment, Grandfather,' he confirmed dryly, still unsure about how he felt about his grandfather having a 'girlfriend'—although he very much doubted, taking into account his grandfather's age, if that term actually applied in this case! Unless of course—

'I hope you're going to remember your manners, laddie,' his grandfather came back darkly. 'I won't have you making any of your clever remarks to—my friend.'

'I'll be on my best behaviour, Grandfather,' Brice promised frowningly; his grandfather must be serious about this woman if he felt this strongly about his family's behaviour in front of her.

Brice wasn't a hundred per cent certain how he felt about that. His grandparents had both been here for all of them when they'd been younger, his grandfather alone for the last few years; he simply couldn't envisage seeing his grandfather with anyone else but his grandmother.

Although that was probably just selfishness on his part, Brice accepted; after all, his grandfather spent most of his time on his own, the rest of them having their own busy lives to lead, when, as his grandfather had pointed out, weeks would go by without any of them giving a thought to visiting him in Scotland.

'You had better be,' came his grandfather's parting comment.

Brice sat in frowning contemplation for several minutes after the call had ended, only forcing himself to move when he realised he had less than an hour to change and drive over to Richard Latham's house. And, after all, what business was it of his whether or not his grandfather had found someone to spend time with? He was over twenty-one—well over!—a widower, and so at liberty to do with his life exactly what he wanted to do with it.

Time to take note of his own advice to Sabina where her mother was concerned, Brice realised; be happy for his grandfather, not judgmental. After all, it was his grandfather's life.

Brice's disappointment was acute when he was shown into Richard Latham's lounge an hour later and found the other man alone there. No doubt Sabina was working again, Brice acknowledged ruefully. Pity.

Richard Latham was dressed formally in a dark grey suit and white shirt, with a discreetly patterned tie of grey and red, blond hair styled short, only a distinctive sprinkling of grey at his temples.

No doubt the latter added to the other man's attractiveness, Brice acknowledged.

And Richard Latham was a handsome man, he accepted disinterestedly, ruggedly attractive, eyes of deep blue, his tall build still lithely fit despite his fifty-odd years.

But as he looked at Richard, Brice realised he disliked the other man intensely!

On first acquaintance Brice had been deeply irritated by

the other man's arrogance, but, looking at him now, Brice
realised his dislike came from a different direction entirely.
This man lived with Sabina, spent every day with her—
every night! Most of all it was those nights that Brice hated
even the thought of, he acknowledged with an inward
shudder!

'Sit down,' Richard invited abruptly. 'Can I offer you a
drink of some kind?' he offered coolly once Brice had
done so. 'Tea? Coffee? Or would you prefer something
stronger?' he drawled.

'No, thanks,' Brice refused as coolly, knowing he
wouldn't be staying long enough to drink anything. Just
being in the same room as this man set his teeth on edge!

The other man looked at him with narrowed blue eyes.
'In that case, what can I do for you?'

Brice's mouth twisted wryly. 'I thought I was the one
who was going to do something for you? Paint Sabina's
portrait,' he added harshly as the other man continued to
look at him with cold enquiry.

'Ah, yes.' Richard nodded slowly, as if just remembering the fact. 'What are your thoughts on that now?'

His antagonism growing by the second, Brice thought
he had better just state his case and leave—as quickly as
possible!

'I'll do it,' he stated flatly. 'But not here. In Scotland.
I—'

'You asked me to let you know when Miss Sabina was
awake, Mr Latham.' The housekeeper had entered the
room after knocking.

'Thank you, Mrs Clark.' Her employer nodded. 'Tell her
I'll be up to see her in a few minutes,' he added dismissively.

'Is Sabina ill?' Brice asked worriedly once the two men
were alone. It was two o'clock in the afternoon, for goodness' sake! Much as he didn't want Sabina to be ill, the
alternative was totally unacceptable!

Something flickered briefly in the other man's eyes at Brice's obvious concern—irritation? Resentment? Displeasure? It was gone too quickly for Brice to tell.

Although there was no doubting that the smile Richard Latham now gave didn't quite reach the icy depths of those pale blue eyes. 'It's nothing,' he dismissed airily. 'Sabina is—delicate. A little nervy, shall we say?' he drawled softly. 'The slightest—disturbance can be quite debilitating for her, poor love.'

The other man seemed to be choosing his words carefully, and yet at the same time Brice felt Richard was also being quite deliberate. And he didn't agree with the other man that Sabina was delicate, or nervy; she seemed a little tense at times, and he wished she smiled more, but other than that she appeared to him to be a woman quite capable of dealing with anything life chose to throw at her. After all, he had been thrown at her—and she had no problem dealing with him!

'I'm sorry to hear that,' Brice answered noncommittally.

Richard Latham gave a slight inclination of his head. 'Sabina has mentioned your idea of going to Scotland to me…'

Brice tensed. 'And?'

The other man shrugged. 'I see no reason why we shouldn't accept your invitation.'

'We'?

Safe in the knowledge the other man would be out of the country, Brice had made that dismissive remark to Sabina about it being a pity that Richard couldn't join them, but it had only been made because Sabina had told him the other man would be in Australia; he hadn't actually meant the invitation to include the other man. Now it looked as if he might have been taken at his word!

Brice sat tensely on the edge of his chair now; having Richard Latham with them in Scotland was the last thing he wanted! 'Sabina led me to believe that you wouldn't be able to make it?'

'Did she?' the other man returned mildly. 'Change of plans,' he dismissed with satisfaction. 'We would both love to join you in Scotland for the weekend.'

So much for the initial impression the other man had given of not knowing the reason for Brice's visit here today!

He gave the other man a narrow-eyed look, not fooled for a moment by Latham's surface charm and refined manners; Richard Latham was every bit as dangerous as his nephew David had warned Brice he could be.

And Sabina was engaged to marry the man!

'Brice has exquisite taste,' Chloe murmured with satisfaction as she slightly adjusted the sash beneath Sabina's breasts, before standing back to admire her work.

Brice was many things, Sabina would have agreed, but a man of taste would be far from the top of her list. Not that the strapless gold gown he had asked Chloe to design for her to wear for the painting of the portrait wasn't absolutely beautiful, because it was; there was just so much more to Brice than the artist.

She had hardly been able to believe it when Richard had informed her that the two men had arranged for all three of them to go up to Scotland this weekend. She had thought, by telling Richard of Brice's suggestion, that he would deal quickly and negatively with the matter; instead Richard had decided to delay his trip to Australia in order to go with her! And without making a scene out of the whole thing, Sabina had been cornered into going along with the plan.

Which was why she had this fitting with Chloe Fox on the day prior to their departure to Scotland!

She'd had the feeling, since first meeting Brice McAllister, of being swept along by the force of a tidal wave—and it wasn't a feeling she found in the least comfortable!

'Do say you like it,' Chloe encouraged now.

It would be impossible not to compliment the other woman on the gown; the material, as Sabina had mockingly suggested to Brice days earlier, was diaphanous gold, her shoulders left completely bare, the material fitting snugly over her breasts, with that sash beneath emphasising the slenderness of her waist, the rest of the gown a floating gold haze down to her bare feet. Sabina was sure she had never worn anything so beautiful.

'It's lovely.' She squeezed the other woman's arm reassuringly.

'Do you think Brice will like it?' Chloe frowned worriedly.

Sabina bit back her tart retort about not caring whether Brice liked it or not, very aware of the fact that, as well as being a very successful fashion designer, Chloe was also married to Brice's cousin, Fergus.

'He's going to love it,' Brice remarked huskily from behind them.

Sabina swung sharply round at the sound of his voice, the colour first flooding and then as quickly receding from her cheeks at the open admiration in Brice's gaze as he looked at her approvingly.

It was only the gown he was admiring and not her personally, she hastily admonished herself. She must try and remember that. The only problem with doing so was that every time she saw Brice things had a habit of becoming very personal indeed!

'I'm so glad you like it,' Chloe said with obvious relief.

'It's perfect,' Brice reassured her as he stepped further into Chloe's fitting-room, dressed in casual denims and a black fitted tee shirt, the latter showing his muscular arms and chest.

Such a startling contrast to how civilised he had looked in black evening clothes!

'You've had your hair cut,' Chloe realised as she looked at him appreciatively.

He had too, Sabina noticed, the over-long dark hair gone in favour of a much shorter style, almost Roman. Somehow it just succeeded in making him appear more ruggedly attractive than ever!

Brice didn't look pleased at Chloe's observation, putting up a self-conscious hand to the darkness of his hair. 'I thought Bohemian was a little out of date,' he drawled self-derisively.

Chloe laughed softly. 'It suited you! I'll just go and rustle us all up some coffee,' she added lightly before leaving the room.

Sabina was very conscious of being left alone with Brice, not quite able to meet the searching gaze she sensed was turned in her direction.

'I'm not quite sure I know how to take Chloe's last remark,' Brice finally murmured dryly.

Sabina didn't believe that for a moment—he knew exactly how to take Chloe's remark; Chloe obviously adored all of her husband's family, would never insult any of them.

Besides, there was no getting away from the fact that Brice was a magnetically attractive man, no matter whether his hair was long or short.

'I'll just go and change back into my own clothes,' Sabina told him huskily, still having trouble looking at him directly.

'That gown is your ''own clothes'',' Brice assured her firmly. 'It will go on Latham's bill for the portrait,' he added with amusement as she raised questioning brows.

'Of course.' She nodded abruptly. 'Nevertheless...' She moved towards the cubicle where she had changed earlier, her normal grace of movement seeming to have deserted her as she bumped into a chair on the way in an effort to avoid walking too close to the immovable Brice.

One of his hands snaked out as she passed, his fingers lightly encircling the top of her arm. 'Are you feeling better now?' he prompted huskily, his gaze searching on the paleness of her face.

'Better...?' She frowned, her brow clearing as she realised he was referring to the fact that she had been in bed when he'd called to see Richard the other day. 'Just a slight tummy disorder,' she excused dismissively.

Brice made no effort to release her, standing very close, the warmth of his breath stirring tendrils of hair at her temple. 'Latham seemed to imply it was something else,' he said slowly.

'You must have misunderstood.' She shook her head, her expression deliberately bland. She had actually received another disturbing letter the particular day Brice was referring to—but she had no intention of him ever knowing about that!

Those green eyes were narrowed as Brice continued to look down at her searchingly. 'No, I don't think so,' he finally murmured softly.

Sabina shrugged dismissively, giving an overbright smile. 'So we're off to Scotland tomorrow,' she deliberately changed the subject.

'So *we* are,' Brice confirmed dryly. 'What's wrong— doesn't Latham trust you to be on your own with me in Scotland for two days?' he added scornfully.

She gave him a derisive look. 'I don't think it's me he doesn't trust,' she returned pointedly.

Brice grinned, a wolfish grin of pure devilment. 'He could be right!' he murmured with satisfaction.

Going on past behaviour, she was sure she was right! Although she also knew she couldn't claim to be completely blameless those times she had been in Brice's arms; somehow she just seemed to find herself there!

And Chloe, Sabina suddenly realised, was taking an awfully long time to prepare the coffee…

'Have you telephoned your mother yet?'

Sabina looked up frowningly at the unexpectedness of Brice's question. 'My mother…?'

He gave an impatient sigh. 'We're going to Scotland. Your mother lives there. Or have you forgotten?' he added hardly.

'Of course I haven't forgotten,' she snapped, at the same time shaking off his restraining hand on her arm. 'But my mother and Richard—' She broke off with an annoyed sigh as she realised what she had been about to say. It was simply none of Brice McAllister's business!

'Your mother and Richard…' Brice repeated thoughtfully. 'Your mother doesn't approve of your aged fiancé!' he guessed triumphantly.

Sabina gave him an impatient grimace. 'Richard isn't "aged",' she defended irritably. 'And there's no law that says my mother has to approve of my choice of fiancé. Or, indeed, vice versa,' she added coolly.

'Latham doesn't like your mother, either,' Brice realised derisively. 'Well, I can quite understand your mother's feelings in the matter; after all, the man is only about ten years younger than she is! But I'll reserve judgement as to whether or not he's right about your mother,' he added dryly.

'You'll "reserve judgement"—' Sabina repeated incredulously. 'Brice, you aren't likely to meet my mother. Besides, none of this has anything to do with you,' she snapped impatiently.

'Nothing at all,' he agreed, stepping back, crossing his arms in front of his chest as he did so. 'Tell me,' he mused softly, 'does anyone like your fiancé? Apart from you, of course,' he added scornfully.

She gasped incredulously. 'Brice, you go too far—'

'Not as far as I would like to go, believe me,' he grated harshly.

Sabina did believe him. That was the trouble. Brice was a law unto himself. Heaven knew what this weekend was going to be like!

She had thought, when Richard had decided he would accompany her, that it would at least solve one problem for her concerning this proposed trip to Scotland; Brice wouldn't be able to just kiss her whenever he felt like it with her fiancé around. But with the unmistakable antagonism from Brice directed towards Richard, she wasn't sure Richard's presence wasn't going to just make the weekend even more unbearable.

If that were possible!

The sooner this portrait was completed and she no longer had to see Brice, the better she would like it!

Where on earth was Chloe with that coffee? More to the point, perhaps, had the other woman known Brice would be calling in here today?

'There is just one other thing about this weekend...' Brice said slowly.

Sabina eyed him warily. 'Yes?'

Brice shrugged. 'My grandfather is in his eighties...'

Her tension increased. 'Yes?'

'This is no moral judgement on your lifestyle, I hope you understand?' He grimaced.

No, Sabina didn't understand—yet. But she had a definite feeling she was very shortly going to!

'Go on,' she invited huskily.

'It's quite simple, really,' Brice continued lightly. 'How you and Latham live when you're in London is your business. But when in Rome—or, in this case, Scotland...' He paused.

'Brice, would you just get to the point?' she snapped, having a feeling that Brice was enjoying this. Whatever 'this' was!

'The point is, Sabina,' he bit out succinctly, 'that my grandfather, being elderly, also has some rather old-fashioned views. And the fact that you and Latham live together when you're in London does not mean my grandfather is willing to accommodate that arrangement when you're in his home! Consequently, you and Latham will be given separate bedrooms during your stay in Scotland,' he concluded with satisfaction.

That was the point!

Sabina could feel the colour suffusing her cheeks, swallowing hard before speaking—she didn't want her voice to come out less than assured. Even if she felt less than assured!

'I'm sure that neither Richard nor I will have a problem with that,' she told him coolly.

Brice's expression darkened. 'I don't give a damn how Latham feels about it. It's you I wanted to save from any embarrassment,' he added grimly.

'How thoughtful of you, Brice,' she said dryly—sure that his actions had nothing to do with kindness. He seemed to spend most of his time embarrassing her in one way or another! 'Now, if you'll excuse me,' she added lightly. 'I really should change out of this gown.' She moved away.

'One other thing, Sabina…' Brice called after her.

She stiffened, turning slowly. 'Yes?' she prompted warily.

His eyes glittered, with amusement, or something else, Sabina couldn't tell. As she couldn't tell too much from his bland tone when he finally spoke, either. 'It's a very old castle, centuries old, and while over the years my grandfather has had a lot of the modern conveniences discreetly installed—'

'You mean it now has indoor plumbing?' Sabina taunted. Blonde brows raised mockingly.

'Amongst other things,' Brice confirmed dryly. 'But I

was actually referring to the fact that my grandfather hasn't had too much success solving the problem of creaking doors and floors,' he concluded challengingly.

Creaking doors and floors—?

Sabina's frowning brow cleared, her cheeks filled with angry colour now as she realised exactly what Brice was intimating; he was warning her that any nocturnal wanderings, by Richard or herself, would in all likelihood be heard by the people in bedrooms close by!

Her gazed was steely as she looked across at him. 'I'm sure that Richard and I can manage to sleep alone for two nights,' she snapped, an angry edge to her tone. 'If that's all…?' she prompted coldly, not waiting for his reply before marching determinedly over to the cubicle and closing the door firmly behind her.

How dared he? How dared he!

Moral judgement on her lifestyle, indeed! Brice knew absolutely nothing about her 'lifestyle' when she lived in London.

Absolutely nothing!

Because if he did, he would already have known that she and Richard had never done anything else *but* occupy separate bedrooms…

CHAPTER TEN

BRICE wished, and not for the first time, that he had accepted Richard Latham's offer to drive himself and Sabina up to Scotland independently of Brice. At the time it had seemed simpler to Brice if they all arrived together; for one thing Latham had no idea, once he reached Scotland, of how to actually get to the castle, and for another, Brice had used the excuse to spend as much time in Sabina's company this weekend as possible. But spending time with Sabina in the company of her fiancé was not a pleasant experience.

Not for Brice, anyway. The other couple seemed to feel no such inhibitions, chatting away together quite happily in the back of Brice's car. Almost as if Brice were superfluous. He might just as well have been the damned chauffeur!

'I hope I'm not driving too fast for you?' he rasped, glancing briefly in the driving mirror—only to find Sabina looking back at him with mockingly raised brows. Almost as if she were well aware of how disgruntled he felt. Minx!

'Not at all,' Richard Latham was the one to dismiss. 'We were just saying we hadn't realised how beautiful it is up here.'

'Honeymoon country,' Brice rasped.

'The Prince and Princess of Wales certainly thought so,' Richard Latham acknowledged dismissively.

'But look what happened to their marriage,' Brice couldn't resist returning caustically.

Richard laughed softly. 'I had the Caribbean more in mind for our honeymoon.'

He would, Brice acknowledged irritably, the thought of

113

Sabina spending a honeymoon anywhere with the other man not exactly improving his mood.

Although another glance in the driving mirror lifted his spirits a little when he saw Sabina was looking at her fiancé with more than a little surprise, giving Brice the impression this was the first she had heard about a honeymoon, in the Caribbean or anywhere else.

In which case, Brice acknowledged slowly, that comment about their honeymoon must have been a direct barb aimed at him...

He straightened in his seat a little at the realisation. He had been wary when Latham had changed his plans and decided to come to Scotland with them, but this last exchange seemed to confirm his suspicion that Richard Latham was aware of Brice's personal interest in Sabina...

Great! Now it seemed his every move this weekend, every word he spoke to Sabina, was going to be under scrutiny.

'My grandfather's estate,' he rasped unwelcomingly as he turned the car into the long driveway that led up to the castle.

'It's beautiful,' Sabina murmured wonderingly a few minutes later, having driven up through the huge herds of deer, the castle itself now in sight.

Brice had been used to staying at his grandfather's castle all his life, knew it as his second home, but that didn't mean he didn't still appreciate the haunting beauty of the castle itself, with its mellow stonework, and huge romantic turrets reaching up into the cloudless sky.

'I believe my fiancée fancies herself as a Lady of the Castle,' Richard Latham drawled a few minutes later as they got out of the parked car, Sabina's pleasure obvious by the look of wonder on her face as she looked around her.

Brice eyed the other man coldly. 'I believe my grandfather is already spoken for,' he returned icily before turning to smile at Sabina, her almost childlike pleasure in her surroundings giving him pleasure too.

'Never mind, Sabina.' Richard Latham put his arm about Sabina's shoulders with light possession. 'If you really want a castle, I can always buy you one.'

Almost as if he were indulging a child with a new bicycle, Brice acknowledged frowningly.

This was not going to be an easy weekend to get through, he realised heavily, when everything the other man said and did irritated him almost to the point of violence. How much more pleasant it would have been if he could have brought Sabina here on her own, sharing the unusual serenity of the family home with her, showing her round, walking the grounds with her, going down to the stream where the family fished for salmon.

'This castle has been in my family for centuries,' he told the other man scathingly.

'Brice is right, Richard.' Sabina spoke huskily. 'This sort of beauty can only be inherited, not bought.'

Brice watched as the other man's mouth tightened fractionally, his obviously having taken exception to the conversation. Or, at least, Sabina's part of it...

'I'm not so sure we inherited it originally,' he told them lightly as he led the way up the stone steps to the huge oak front door. 'I believe one of our ancestors claimed it for his own after being involved in a raid where the original owner was killed!'

'The Scots have always loved a fight, haven't they?' Richard Latham said mildly.

Too mildly, as far as Brice was concerned, sure that there had been a double edge to the other man's remark. Well, if the other man thought he was about to give him a fight over Sabina, he was wrong; Sabina was an independent woman of twenty-five, not a possession for two men to fight over as if she were the prize!

'We have been known to dispose of the odd unwanted

Sassenach,' his grandfather was the one to dryly answer the other man as he stood silhouetted in the now open doorway, light streaming out welcomingly from inside the castle.

'Grandfather!' Brice smiled as he moved forward to give his eldest relative the customary hug.

'So you've arrived at last, laddie,' his grandfather rebuked as he stood back. 'Although I might be persuaded into forgiving you for delaying dinner—' his eyes gleamed admiringly as he turned his attention to Sabina '—if you will introduce me to this beautiful young lady,' he added charmingly.

'Sabina,' she huskily introduced herself as she held out her hand, looking beautiful, as Brice's grandfather had just said, in a fitted black dress, her hair gleaming pure gold as it flowed down over her shoulders to her waist. 'And I'm afraid I'm the one you have to blame for our tardiness,' she added with a grimace. 'I had a little trouble deciding what I would need to pack for a weekend in Scotland.'

Brice's grandfather had retained a hold on her hand, tucking it securely into the crook of his arm now as he turned to take her inside. 'I'm sure you always look beautiful whatever you wear,' he told her gallantly.

Brice shot Richard Latham a sideways glance, not altogether sure he liked the look of derision on the other man's face as he watched Hugh walk away with his fiancée. 'Help me carry the luggage in, Latham,' he instructed harshly, opening up the boot of the car, at the same time sure that the other man wasn't accustomed to carrying his own luggage.

A learning experience for him, then, Brice decided hardly. His grandfather employed several household staff, and the castle was run with extreme efficiency by all of them, but that didn't mean Richard Latham could expect a free ride this weekend. No matter what he might be used to!

Brice came to a halt in the doorway of the sitting-room a few minutes later, after delivering the luggage to the bedrooms, as he heard Sabina laughing with his grandfather. It was a huskily girlish sound, completely uninhibited.

'Sorry,' Richard Latham rasped as, given no warning of Brice's sudden stop, he walked straight into his back. 'What's the hold-up, McAllister?' he prompted mockingly.

The 'hold-up' was the complete novelty, to Brice, of hearing Sabina laugh!

It was a wonderful sound, deep and natural, hinting at a slightly wicked sense of humour if allowed free rein. As it was now, Sabina's cheeks flushed, her eyes bright, as she obviously enjoyed her conversation with Brice's grandfather.

'Well, don't just dawdle in the doorway, laddie,' his grandfather instructed lightly as he looked up and saw Brice standing there. 'Make yourself useful and offer our guests a drink.'

Brice was used to his grandfather treating him as if he were still six years old, but he could see that Sabina was enjoying the novelty of it, that smile still lurking about her mouth and eyes as she looked across at him.

Brice felt some of the tension he had known on the journey here ease, suddenly feeling, as he saw how relaxed Sabina was with his grandfather, that it was going to be an okay weekend after all—with or without the presence of Richard Latham!

'What would you like to drink, Sabina?' Brice offered dryly as he moved to the array of drinks that stood on top of a glass cabinet. 'It seems we have white or red wine.' He scrutinised the bottles. 'Gin. Vodka. Or there's whisky, if you would prefer it.'

No doubt, being in Scotland, the men would be drinking

whisky, Sabina acknowledged ruefully, opting for the white wine herself; she had never been particularly keen on strong spirits.

'Isn't this wonderful?' she prompted Richard as he crossed the room to sit down next to her on the sofa.

'Wonderful,' he echoed, with a definite lack of enthusiasm—to Sabina, at least—in his voice.

She gave him a frowning look. Richard couldn't possibly not like this place. It was the most beautiful home she had ever seen, the furniture obviously all antique, suits of armour, swords and helmets, adorning the mellow stone walls. She had even seen a cannon at the bottom of one of the staircases that obviously led up to the turret bedrooms.

Visions of Rapunzel, she had teased Brice last week when he'd made the suggestion of their coming here so he could paint her. But now that she was here Sabina could see exactly why he had found the idea so intriguing. The castle was enchanting, like something out of a fairy story!

'It's very remote here,' Richard remarked as Brice handed him his requested glass of whisky. 'And it must cost you a fortune in heating bills.'

Hugh McDonald's eyes narrowed. 'The remoteness means we aren't bothered too much by nosy sightseers,' he rasped pointedly. 'And if you have to count the cost then you can't afford to live here,' he added dryly.

Richard's practical remark had given the air a certain tension that hadn't been there a couple of minutes ago, Sabina realised regretfully. She was sure Richard hadn't intended any insult, but at the same time she was aware that one had been taken.

'I thought we were to be five for dinner this evening, Grandfather?' Brice remarked lightly as he sat in one of the chairs opposite.

Hugh gave him a steely look. 'My guest will be arriving tomorrow,' he answered abruptly.

'I'm looking forward to it,' Brice returned with relish.

Sabina looked at each of the two men, sensing something in the conversation that neither she nor Richard were aware of. But then, why should they be? Hugh and Brice had a relationship that had existed long before, and was completely separate from, this weekend.

'Could I possibly go upstairs and freshen up before dinner?' She turned to smile at Hugh as she put down her wineglass. 'I feel a little dusty from travelling.'

'You see, Brice, I've been telling you for years to get yourself a decent car,' his grandfather taunted, the teasing obviously a regular thing between the two men; Brice's black Mercedes was obviously a top-of-the-range model, the last word in luxury.

Brice shook his head, standing up. 'I shall treat that remark with the contempt it so obviously deserves,' he dismissed before turning to Sabina. 'I'll take you upstairs and show you your room,' he told her huskily.

She should have realised that Brice would be the one to take her up to her bedroom, Sabina admonished herself as she stood up to follow him. She should have done. But she hadn't.

She had promised herself before leaving London earlier today that she would make every effort to be alone with Brice as little as possible this weekend. And within minutes of their arrival she found herself exactly that!

'Don't be long, Sabina,' Richard told her softly as she reached the doorway. 'I'm sure we've delayed Mr McDonald's dinner enough already this evening.'

'Mr McDonald,' Sabina mused as she followed Brice out into the hallway. Strange, she had found no difficulty in calling the elderly man Hugh from the moment he'd asked her to do so. Except…he hadn't offered Richard the same intimacy.

Just an oversight, she decided. After all, she had been with Hugh the whole time the two men had been taking the luggage upstairs, whereas Richard had only just joined them.

'Mind yourself on the narrowness of the stairs,' Brice warned as she followed him up the stone steps.

It was a timely warning, Sabina having to hold onto the rope on the wall that acted as a banister several times as they negotiated the narrow winding of the staircase.

'After London this is like a different world,' she said almost dazedly, feeling as if she had been picked up and placed in a time warp.

Bruce turned at the top of the stairs to wait for her. 'You'll find the "indoor plumbing" perfectly satisfactory,' he assured her dryly.

Sabina felt the colour in her cheeks as he reminded her of her mockery the day before. Trust Brice to throw that remark back at her! She decided not to qualify the remark with an answer.

Although she did make a mental note to be more careful in future what she did say to Brice. If she could be any more careful than she already was!

Sabina had never seen a circular bedroom before, the luxuriously furnished room Brice showed her into decorated in warm cream and golds.

But it was the narrow windows that intrigued her, and she hurried to each of them in turn to look out at the three-hundred-and-sixty-degree views still visible in the fading light of evening: a forest to one side, a lake to another, walled gardens to another, and the herds of deer grazing to the front of the castle.

'If I lived somewhere like this I would never want to leave,' she breathed wonderingly.

'If you lived here, neither would I,' Brice answered huskily from just behind her.

Far too close behind her, Sabina discovered as she swung round, finding herself almost pressed against his chest, becoming very still, her breathing shallow.

It was as if time were standing still as they looked at each other in the twilight, Brice's face vividly clear to her, his eyes a sparkling emerald-green, the intimacy of his words laying heavily between them.

She should stop this, break the spell—except that was exactly what it felt like, as if she were bewitched, by both Brice and her surroundings.

'I had better rejoin the others,' he finally murmured gruffly.

'Yes,' she confirmed. But she wasn't altogether surprised when he made no effort to do so.

A nerve pulsed in his jaw as he continued to look at her, the very air between them seeming to crackle with an unspoken awareness.

'You really should go down now,' Sabina told him huskily.

He sighed. 'Yes.'

But still he didn't do so, neither moving away nor reaching out to touch her. Just standing there.

He drew in a ragged breath. 'Sabina—'

'Go, Brice,' she cut in softly. 'Please!' she added firmly before he could say anything else.

His mouth tightened. 'Yes.' He nodded abruptly, stepping back. 'I'll see you downstairs in a few minutes,' he added before finally leaving the bedroom.

Sabina didn't move, couldn't move, clasping her hands together in front of her to stop them shaking. What was happening to her?

No—not what was happening to her; what had already happened to her?

She was engaged to marry Richard, had so much to be grateful to him for, knew that she was safe with him. And yet she had just made a discovery that threatened to put all of that in jeopardy.

She had fallen in love with Brice McAllister!

CHAPTER ELEVEN

'FOR goodness' sake relax, Sabina,' Brice rasped impatiently as he looked at her over the top of the canvas he was working on. 'I've already eaten this morning; I'm not about to gobble you up as an after-breakfast treat!' he added disgustedly.

They had been working on the portrait barely half an hour, Sabina standing stiffly across the room from him, wearing the shimmering gold gown, turned slightly away as she looked wistfully out of the window. And not once during that thirty minutes had Sabina been what Brice would have described as relaxed.

When in reality he should be the one who couldn't relax—because when he sat back and glanced across at Sabina it was to see only her head and shoulders, alluringly bare shoulders that conjured up visions in his head of her completely naked.

'I didn't think you were,' she answered him dryly now. 'It's just—I'm a little cold,' she dismissed awkwardly.

A little cold! Brice would have described it as more than that. Since she'd rejoined the three men before going in to dinner the previous evening, Sabina's whole attitude had bordered on the icy, and it had remained that way. Towards him, at least...

He shouldn't have lingered last night having taken her to her bedroom, he acknowledged that; he just hadn't been able to drag himself away. She had just looked so right in that setting, so absolutely perfect; and the realisation had very little to do with painting her in these surroundings!

One positive thing to have come out of her obvious coolness towards him: Richard Latham, basking in the warmth of Sabina's attentions, had become quite convivial company as dinner had progressed, showing a relaxed, charming side of him that Brice, for one, would rather not have seen—it was probably the side of him that Sabina loved!

It certainly hadn't succeeded in encouraging Brice to like Richard Latham any better, and he had seen his grandfather shooting the other man a couple of narrow-eyed glances of speculation during the evening too.

The fact that his grandfather didn't seem to like the other man either had cheered him a little—perhaps his own dislike wasn't so misplaced, after all? But only a little, Brice having wished the evening and night over so that he could once again be alone with Sabina.

But with Sabina still in this coolly remote mood, it wasn't turning out to be much fun!

He stood up abruptly. 'Your heart really isn't in this, is it?' he rasped impatiently. 'Even for Latham's sake,' he added scornfully.

Sabina looked away. 'If I could just have the window closed…?'

'Why not?' He strode across the room and slammed the window shut with barely repressed violence, drawing in a deeply controlling breath before turning back to her, realising that his tension was becoming as acute as her own. 'What is it, Sabina?' he prompted gently.

She took a step back. 'I—you didn't—explain, that the room you wanted to paint me in was your bedroom!' she burst out accusingly, her cheeks bright red, whether with temper or embarrassment Brice wasn't sure.

So that was it! This morning, at least…

Brice shrugged. 'This isn't just my bedroom when I'm here; it's also my studio.' Obviously, with all his canvases and paints about the room.

Although, he supposed—and he had never really thought about it before!—it must seem a little strange with his double bed in the room too… He had never thought of it—because he had never had a woman in his 'studio' here before. For any reason.

His mouth twisted derisively. 'Latham wouldn't like it, hmm?' he scorned.

Sabina's eyes flashed deeply blue. 'I don't like it,' she corrected firmly.

'Why don't you?' he taunted.

She moved sharply across the room to stare out the window that looked towards the lake. 'It's so peaceful here…' she murmured almost to herself.

Brice looked across at her with narrowed eyes. 'You haven't answered my question,' he rasped determinedly.

Sabina glanced back at him, the frown having eased from between her brows as she'd gazed outside. 'Because I don't believe it needs answering,' she told him softly.

He drew in a sharp breath. 'Sabina—'

'Where has your grandfather taken Richard this morning?' she prompted lightly.

To the top of a mountain and pushed him off, for all Brice cared! Although he didn't for a moment think it was something his grandfather would do. Or that it was a reply Sabina would care for.

'I believe they went for a drive round the estate,' he dismissed uninterestedly. 'Don't worry, Sabina, I'm sure you'll see your fiancé again soon,' he added tauntingly.

She shook her head. 'I'm not worried,' she assured him dryly.

Not about that, anyway, Brice acknowledged frowningly. But she was troubled about something…

'Sabina, if you don't tell me what's wrong, how can I help you?' he said gently.

She gave him an incredulous glance. 'I don't remember saying there was anything wrong! Neither do I remember asking for your help!' she added dismissively.

'But you obviously need someone's help,' he bit out impatiently. 'So why not mine?'

Sabina shook her head. 'I have no idea what you're talking about, Brice. And if I should have any worries,' she continued firmly as he would have spoken, 'I have a fiancé, and a mother, I can discuss them with, as necessary.'

And not with the relative stranger who happened to have taken the liberty of kissing her a couple of times, her words clearly implied!

He shrugged. 'I had the distinct impression you don't have that sort of relationship with your mother. Did you call her, by the way, to tell her you're in Scotland for the weekend?'

Sabina's mouth tightened impatiently at this sudden veer in the conversation. 'You're very persistent, Brice,' she snapped.

'Well?' He raised dark, uncompromising brows.

'No, I didn't,' she answered irritably.

'Why the hell not?' he rasped.

She shrugged. 'Scotland is a big place—'

'Where does your mother live?' Brice snapped, his mouth twisting angrily as she named a village only five miles away. 'Sabina—'

'Will you just leave it, Brice?' She moved impatiently, returning to her position across the room. 'I thought we came here so you could paint,' she added pointedly.

'I could always try telephoning her myself; there can't be too many Smiths in this area,' Brice said dryly.

Sabina glared angrily. 'You could always try minding your own business!'

He held up his hands defensively. 'I'm only trying to help, Sabina.'

'And I've just told you I don't need your help,' she returned with displeasure. 'My relationship with my mother is my business, Brice, not yours,' she rasped.

'Or not. As the case may be…' he said softly.

'Oh, this is hopeless!' Sabina threw up her hands in disgust before marching over to the door. 'I need some fresh air,' she bit out tersely. 'We can resume this later,' she added in a tone of voice that brooked no argument.

It was a tone that even Brice knew he would be wise to take note of!

What was the saying, it was always the quiet ones to watch out for…? Sabina, for the most part, was coolly self-possessed, seemingly completely unruffled, but the last few minutes had shown him there was also another side to her; Sabina, if pushed too far, came out fighting!

On balance, Brice decided it was a trait he rather liked…

What a disaster! What an absolute mess, Sabina muttered to herself as she changed out of the gold gown into a pink tee shirt and denims, fully intending to go ahead with her avowal of needing some air.

She straightened from putting on her sandals, breathing deeply. What was she going to do? What could she do?

She was engaged to Richard, a man who had never shown her anything but kindness and concern, and she was in love with Brice, a man who— Who what? A man who had also shown her kindness and concern. In his own way.

But Brice had shown her something else, given her a realisation of her own capacity for passion that, until meeting him, she hadn't known existed.

How could this have happened to her?

Last November she had been deeply upset, her self-confidence in shreds because of what had happened. Richard had already been a friend, she'd occasionally had dinner with, and having seen her obvious distress he had made his suggestion that, for their mutual benefit—Sabina for Richard's protection, Richard because he liked the idea of being seen with the most photographed model in the

world—the two of them become engaged, it hadn't taken
Sabina too long to decide that she liked the idea, too.

But she hadn't realised when she'd come to that understanding with Richard that she was capable of loving
someone in the way she now loved Brice. If she had
thought for a moment she could ever feel this way about
another man she would never have accepted Richard's
kind offer.

Sabina had gone round and round in her head with these
same thoughts as she'd lain in bed the previous evening
unable to sleep, wondering what to do next.

One thing she did realise…she had to tell Richard how
she felt, knew she could no longer go on being engaged
to him, taking advantage of his kindness, sharing his home
with him, when she had these feelings, longings, for another man.

And she had no idea how to go about telling Richard
that!

If she had known, even partially guessed, how this
weekend was going to change her life, then she would
have run as fast and as far as she could in the other direction.

And being alone with Brice in his bedroom-studio, with
her newly discovered feelings towards him, had been absolute torture.

She stood up, tired of her own company too now; it was
too easy to just sit and think when she was alone.

The gardens, the ones she could see from her bedroom
window. She would go there. Anywhere, to get away from
Brice!

And maybe, by the time she had taken a leisurely stroll
through the gardens, Hugh and Richard would have returned from their drive. Although the thought of seeing
Richard, with her emotions in such confusion, wasn't particularly appealing, either. Because she knew, instinctively,

that he was not going to be pleased with what she had to say to him…

Oh, damn Brice McAllister. She wished she had never met him.

'Going for a walk?'

Sabina turned sharply as, having reached the bottom of the stairs in preparation of escaping, she found herself confronted with Hugh McDonald as he came out of a room at the end of the hallway.

'Richard has borrowed the car to drive to the village and pick up a newspaper,' Hugh supplied the answer to the question Sabina had just been about to ask.

She smiled indulgently. 'He hates it if he misses the business section even for one day.'

Hugh nodded. 'So he said. If you're going for a walk, would you like some company?' he prompted gently.

She would love some company, anything to escape her own tumultuous thoughts. But… 'I'm sure we've already disturbed your routine enough for one day,' she excused.

'Not in the least,' the elderly man dismissed with a smile. 'A man of my age never minds being disturbed by a beautiful woman!'

Sabina laughed, not because she knew she was meant to, but because she genuinely found Hugh's teasing refreshing after the intensity of emotion of the last twelve hours. 'In that case—' she linked her arm in the crook of his '—I would love it if you would accompany me on my walk.'

'Where would you like to go?' Hugh prompted once they were outside in the late May sunshine, blossom on the trees, birds singing amongst their branches.

'I've had a thing about walled gardens ever since I read about one being brought back to life in one of the books I read as a child,' she admitted guilelessly.

Hugh grinned down at her, looking much younger than his eighty-odd years. 'I think I must have read the same book,' he acknowledged conspiratorially. 'Although we don't do as much with those gardens any more,' he added sadly. 'It was my wife who liked to cultivate them, you see.'

Sabina had already realised that he was a widower of some years' standing. 'That's a pity,' she murmured softly.

'Yes,' he acknowledged thoughtfully. 'Actually, Sabina, I'm quite pleased to have this time alone with you.' Hugh looked down at her with quizzical eyes. 'Tell me—from a young female point of view—do you think my family is likely to want to have me committed if I tell them I've fallen in love again, at my age?'

Her eyes widened in alarm at the sudden intimacy of the unexpected question. 'I'm not sure—I don't—erm—'

'Sorry.' Hugh chuckled at her obvious surprise, shaking his head self-derisively, 'I didn't mean to shock you.'

'You didn't,' Sabina assured him, feeling embarrassed now at the stupidity of her own reaction.

'I just wanted someone else's opinion before broaching the subject with any of the family.' Hugh frowned. 'Although I think Brice already has an idea...' He grimaced.

Brice would, Sabina thought irritably, preceding Hugh into the first walled garden as he held the door open for her, instantly enchanted by the profusion of wild flowers whose sight and perfume assailed her senses.

'So what do you think?' Hugh prompted softly.

Her eyes shone with pleasure as she looked around her. 'It's beautiful! Exactly as I would have imagined it—'

'I was actually referring to our earlier conversation,' Hugh corrected dryly.

Which she had no idea how to answer! Hugh, despite being in his eighties, was still an attractive man; so why shouldn't he fall in love, at this age or any other? But, on the other hand, in view of her own reaction to her mother being involved with someone, she could see how Hugh's family might be more than a little surprised by his news...

'I can clearly see men in white coats and bars at the windows in your eyes!' Hugh murmured self-derisively.

'Not at all.' Sabina laughed throatily. 'You've just put me in something of a dilemma, that's all,' she admitted ruefully. 'You see, I've just encountered something—similar, in my own life, where my widowed mother is concerned,' she confided softly.

Hugh looked at her with narrowed eyes. 'And?'

She grimaced. 'I didn't react too well, I'm afraid,' she admitted regretfully.

'Ah.'' Hugh nodded.

'Indeed,' Sabina sighed. 'My only advice to you would be not to take too much notice of initial reactions.'

He raised silver brows. 'Meaning yours wasn't too good where your mother was concerned?' he guessed shrewdly.

She gave a self-conscious laugh. 'Meaning my reaction was pretty awful,' she admitted with regret.

After all, was her mother finding someone else to share the otherwise loneliness of life such a terrible thing? In view of the mess Sabina's own life had become in the last twelve hours, the realisation that she was engaged to one man while finding herself deeply attracted to another one, to the point of knowing herself in love with him, she was inclined to think not.

'Tell me, Sabina,' Hugh began slowly, watching her with thoughtful curiosity. 'What do you think of my grandson?'

Her eyes widened at this next sharp turn in their conversation. 'Which one?' she delayed awkwardly.

Hugh smiled. 'You've met Logan and Fergus, too?'

'Only Fergus. We—' She broke off abruptly; how would it sound to this elderly man if she told him she and Brice had had dinner with the McClouds? 'But I've seen Logan,' she continued slightly breathlessly. 'They look very alike, don't they?' she dismissed lightly.

'They are alike.' Hugh nodded. 'McDonalds, every one. I made sure of that,' he added firmly.

And he was obviously proud of each and every one of them. With good reason; each of the men, besides being extremely attractive, was very successful in his chosen field.

'But you didn't answer my question about Brice, Sabina?' Hugh persisted, his gaze narrowed assessingly.

'I think,' she avoided teasingly, 'that Brice gets his bluntness from his grandfather!'

The elderly man chuckled with pleasure. 'I brought them up to believe that honesty is always the best policy—even if you end up making a few enemies along the way. And talking of honesty,' he began slowly. 'Sabina—'

'Hello, there.' Richard calling to them from the open doorway of the garden interrupted what Hugh had been about to say.

For which Sabina was more than grateful; she hadn't known what she would have said if Hugh had persisted along this line of questions concerning her feelings towards Brice! The realisation of her love for Brice was still too new, the whole situation too raw to emotional turmoil, that she didn't want to even think about it just now, let alone talk about Brice!

Although she wasn't sure she felt ready to face Richard at the moment, either...

'Look who I just met outside,' Richard told them lightly as he stepped to one side to reveal someone standing behind him in the garden doorway.

Sabina found herself looking at her own mother!

What—?

Sabina looked at her mother frowningly, totally bewildered at the suddenness of her appearance here, of all places. If Brice had dared to carry out that threat to telephone her mother—

'Joan...' Hugh croaked gruffly.

Sabina turned to look at him, only to find that Hugh looked more than a little uncomfortable himself at this sudden turn of events, embarrassed even, a flush of those ruddy cheeks, anxiety in the deep blue of his eyes.

And then the truth hit Sabina with the force of a blow between the eyes.

Hugh had talked to her of having recently fallen in love.

Her mother had done something similar when they'd met in London for lunch last week.

Hugh McDonald, Brice's grandfather, was the man in her mother's life!

CHAPTER TWELVE

'SABINA, I think you're totally overreacting—'

'I didn't ask for your opinion!' She turned harshly on Brice as he sat on the side of her bed watching as she threw clothes haphazardly into the suitcase beside him. 'In fact, in the circumstances, I think the best thing you can do is not to say a single word on the subject!' She glared at him angrily, eyes glittering deeply blue, her whole body tense with repressed fury.

Some of which, Brice conceded grimly, she was perfectly entitled to feel.

He had arrived downstairs a few minutes ago, just in time to see Sabina come storming through the front doorway, hot wings of temper in the usual paleness of her cheeks.

'What on earth—?'

'Leave her, Brice,' his grandfather had instructed harshly as he'd followed closely behind Sabina.

'But—'

'I said leave her!' his grandfather rasped coldly, both men standing in the hallway watching Sabina before she disappeared round the curve of the stairs.

Brice turned back to his grandfather. 'What on earth is going on?' he demanded to know; Sabina might be in some strange sort of mood with him, but she had seemed to like his grandfather well enough last night. 'What have you done to Sabina?' he prompted accusingly.

Something flickered in his grandfather's gaze, an emotion he quickly masked, although his expression remained grim. 'I haven't *done* anything to her, laddie,' he grated, his accent all the stronger because of his own repressed anger. 'At least—' he frowned '—nothing deliberately designed to hurt or upset her.'

'You seem to have succeeded in doing both,' Brice pointed out tersely, torn between a desire to run after Sabina, and the need to stand here and hear what his grandfather had to say.

His grandfather held up defensive hands. 'It seemed like an act of providence when you told me you were bringing Sabina here this weekend.' He shook his head. 'But, unfortunately, before I had time to explain the situation to her—'

'Go back a step, Grandfather,' Brice cut in evenly. 'What was providential about my bringing Sabina here...?' He frowned his wariness of the possible answer.

Although he couldn't for the life of him think what that answer might be. As far as he was aware Sabina and his grandfather had never met before, so what could the elderly man possibly have needed to explain to her...?

'I think I might better be able to answer that for you,' a calm, female voice remarked from the direction of the doorway.

Brice turned frowningly. A tiny blonde-haired woman stood there, a woman probably aged in her sixties, despite the shoulder-length of her hair, the pretty face and slenderness of her figure. A woman Brice knew he had never seen before.

And yet...

As he looked at her he realised there was something tantalisingly familiar about the deep blue of her eyes, those high cheekbones, and the creaminess of her skin...

Sabina had said she looked like her father, and yet here was clear evidence that wasn't completely true...

Brice drew in a ragged breath. 'I see.'

The woman tilted her head engagingly to one side. 'Do you?'

'I believe so.' Brice nodded slowly, turning back to his grandfather. 'Why didn't you tell me?'

Because it was more than obvious to Brice now that it was Sabina's mother who was his grandfather's 'friend'.

Was it any wonder that Sabina was upset?

His grandfather moved to put a protective arm about the shoulders of the woman Brice only knew as Sabina's mother. 'Joan didn't exactly have a pleasant time of it when she tried to tell Sabina about us the other week,' his grandfather rasped. 'You young people seem to think you have some sort of monopoly when it comes to falling in love!' he added disgustedly.

'Excuse me.' Richard Latham spoke icily from behind the older couple, stepping into the hallway as they moved to one side. 'Is Sabina upstairs?' he prompted curtly.

'She is,' Brice confirmed grimly; he had been wondering where the other man had got to!

Richard Latham nodded abruptly. 'Sabina and I will be leaving shortly. We'll need a taxi to drive us to the nearest airport,' he added arrogantly.

'I'll drive you,' Brice told him coldly.

Richard Latham gave him a scathing glance. 'I don't think so. But if you could see to the ordering of the taxi…?' He gave a dismissive nod before following Sabina up the stairs.

Almost as if he were some sort of hired help. Brice fumed angrily, finding himself wanting to follow the other man up the stairs and punch him squarely in the face!

'Richard doesn't like me, I'm afraid.' Joan Smith spoke ruefully. 'I've been a little too outspoken concerning his suitability as a fiancé for Sabina,' she admitted with a grimace.

'In that case—' Brice turned back to the quietly spoken woman '—I like you very much!' he told her with satisfaction.

Joan laughed huskily, a laugh so like Sabina's, Brice felt an ache in his chest just at the sound of it.

Sabina…

What must she be feeling? More to the point, what must she be thinking?

'I have to go up and talk to Sabina,' he told the older couple distractedly. 'Before Latham has a chance to add his particular brand of poison to the confusion,' he added harshly.

'You're wasting your time, I'm afraid,' her mother told him sadly. 'In the last few months I've watched my beautiful, self-confident daughter turn into someone I hardly recognise.' She shook her head regretfully.

Brice looked at her frowningly, wanting to pursue the subject, but at the same time knowing he had to speak to Sabina. Now.

'Hold that thought,' Brice told Joan forcefully. 'And don't go away before I have a chance to talk to you again,' he urged even as he began to ascend the stone stairs two at a time.

'Joan isn't going anywhere,' his grandfather assured him firmly.

Brice hadn't been sure whether he'd been relieved or disappointed when he'd entered Sabina's bedroom a few minutes later to find her alone; half of him had still been hoping to actually carry out his urge to hit Richard Latham. Although, in the circumstances, that probably wasn't such a good idea at the moment…

'Sabina,' he tried again now, 'is it really so awful that my grandfather and your mother have become—friends?' he concluded awkwardly, having no idea how far the relationship between the older couple had progressed. Although the two of them did intend holidaying in Paris together.

Sabina resumed throwing her clothes into the suitcase. 'I told you I don't want to talk about it!' she snapped.

Brice frowned. 'Is that the way you usually deal with things nowadays—bury your head in the sand and hope they'll go away?' he challenged.

She looked at him with narrowed eyes. '"Nowadays"…?' she repeated warily.

He shrugged. 'Your mother seems to be of the opinion that you've changed since you became engaged to Latham.' Brice saw no harm in trying to get a few answers himself as to the reason for the change in her that Joan had noticed.

'Really?' Sabina dismissed with a shrug. 'I've already told you that my mother and Richard don't like each other.'

Implying her mother was simply prejudiced in her opinion. Except that Brice found he didn't believe that of the woman he had just met downstairs…

He was still amazed at the fact that his grandfather and Sabina's mother had somehow found each other and apparently fallen in love. The chances of that happening had to be incredible.

But was it any more incredible than the way he felt towards Sabina?

Also, it was strange, but with the knowledge that it was Sabina's mother his grandfather was seeing Brice found he no longer felt that instinctive rejection of such a relationship in the older man's life.

Whereas Sabina obviously felt the opposite!

But how much of that was directed towards the unsuitability of his grandfather as a suitor to her mother, and how much was it because it happened to be Brice's grandfather?

'Won't you give them a chance, Sabina?' he prompted gently. 'After all, they're both adults, and—' He broke off as Sabina turned on him fiercely, looking up at him with widened eyes.

'Don't you understand, I can't think about this just now?' she grated emotionally.

Brice studied her more closely. Was that tears he could see in her eyes, building up against the lashes as they threatened to fall?

'Sabina!' He stood up abruptly, reaching out to take her into his arms. 'It will be all right, you'll see,' he told her soothingly as he cradled her head against his shoulder.

It would never be all right again!

How could it be, when she had fallen in love with Brice while engaged to Richard, and now she found her mother was involved with Brice's grandfather? That relationship alone made it impossible for her to distance herself from Brice—or his family!

She had thought last night, once she'd realised her feelings towards Brice, that this situation couldn't get any worse. With her mother's arrival it just had!

'Sabina…?' Brice prompted huskily now as he looked down at her concernedly.

She loved this man, every arrogant, attractive, caring inch of him. What was she going to do?

Brice looked at her searchingly, those emerald-coloured eyes like penetrating jewels. She only hoped he couldn't see what was in her heart!

'Sabina…' he finally groaned throatily, pressing her closer to his chest before his head lowered and his lips claimed hers.

Heaven.

Absolute, complete heaven.

Her arms moved up instinctively about his shoulders as she returned the kiss, senses raging as pleasure coursed through her, her lips parting invitingly beneath his.

Brice accepted that invitation with a low growl in his throat, the kiss instantly deepening as his mouth crushed hers, the warmth of his tongue moving sensually against hers.

Sabina clung to the broad width of his shoulders even as her body curved itself instinctively into the hardness of his, able to feel every muscle and sinew, his own arousal unmistakable.

Her neck arched as Brice's lips moved from hers to trail a blaze of fire down the sensitive column of her throat, his tongue now caressing the deep hollows at its base, one of his hands moving to cup the pertness of her breast against the thin material of her tee shirt.

She gave a gasp of pure pleasure as his thumbtip moved lightly over the hardened tip of her nipple, her legs feeling weak as hot desire swept through her entire body, her panting breath sounding loud in the otherwise quiet of the bedroom.

'Brice…!' she groaned achingly, knowing she wanted more, so much more.

'This is right, Sabina,' he muttered forcefully against the lobe of her ear. 'So very, very right!' His arms tightened painfully about her.

'I—' She broke off abruptly, hearing another noise that she somehow knew—even in her befuddled state of arousal—wasn't made by either Brice or herself.

She quickly pulled back from Brice, pushing against his chest, just managing to free herself from his arms and step away from him as the bedroom door opened, Sabina's sharp glance in that direction showing her that Richard stood there.

Her fiancé!

She felt her cheeks blushing painfully red as she looked guiltily across at the man whose ring nestled on her left hand, wondering if Richard knew, if he guessed, if there was anything about Brice and herself that showed that only seconds ago they had been in each other's arms.

It was impossible to tell anything of Richard's emotions

from his deadpan expression as he looked at them, the blue eyes narrowed speculatively, but not accusingly.

He arched blond brows. 'Are we still leaving?' he drawled interestedly.

'We are.' Sabina gave an abrupt nod of her head, moving to close her suitcase, all the time keeping her gaze averted from Brice as he stood tensely only feet away from her, hands clenched at his sides. If he dared to say anything that would imply—!

'In the circumstances, McAllister, I think it's probably best if we don't go ahead with the portrait, after all,' Richard addressed the other man dryly.

'Circumstances?' Brice echoed harshly.

Richard shrugged. 'Sabina is obviously—upset, by her mother's friendship with your grandfather,' he dismissed derisively.

'Are you?' Brice rasped in her direction.

Sabina slowly raised her head, reluctantly meeting Brice's probing gaze. 'I—I'm not sure how I feel about that at the moment,' she answered honestly, needing time and space to digest the fact before knowing how she felt about it. 'But I do agree with Richard that it would be best if we leave now, that it's better to forget about the portrait, too,' she added firmly.

Brice's mouth thinned angrily. 'Why?'

Because she daredn't be alone in a room with him! Because every time she looked at him she wanted him, shamelessly, unreservedly, completely! Because she loved him!

Because there was no point in the portrait being painted when she was going to end her engagement to Richard…!

She shook her head dismissively. 'As you're well aware, I was never interested in having the portrait done in the first place,' she reminded distantly.

'You only went ahead with it to please your fiancé, is that it?' Brice rasped scornfully.

Sabina's head went back proudly at the open challenge in his words. 'That's it exactly,' she confirmed tersely, a certain defiance in her gaze now as she met Brice's unblinkingly, knowing she was daring him to dispute her words, but unable to do anything about it.

Brice's mouth turned back contemptuously. 'I'm sure there must be many other ways in which you can "please" your fiancé,' he taunted scathingly.

'I'm sure there are,' Sabina returned coldly, not liking the tone in Brice's voice at all.

'Just send me a bill for whatever time and materials you've already used,' Richard told the other man dismissively.

The emerald eyes hardened to angry pebbles of light. 'That won't be necessary,' Brice rasped.

'But I always take care of my debts, Brice,' Richard told him smoothly.

'I said, forget it,' Brice snapped harshly.

Sabina anxiously watched the exchange between the two men. Looking at Brice now, it was hard to believe that only minutes ago they had been in each other's arms, totally lost in their arousal, everyone and everything else forgotten. Brice now looked coldly remote, and she—

Sabina didn't know how she looked, only knew she had to get away from here, away from Brice, away from the spell this place seemed to have cast over her! Back to London where she knew who she was and where she was going.

'If you're ready to leave now, Sabina?' Richard prompted pointedly, obviously bored by his conversation with the other man.

'I'm ready.' She reached out to swing her zipped suitcase onto the floor.

'I'm sure Brice isn't going to be so petty as to let you carry your own suitcase downstairs. Are you, McAllister?'

Richard taunted challengingly as he picked up his own packed suitcase.

'No,' Brice rasped tersely, abruptly relieving Sabina of her burden, his fingers, briefly, icily cold against hers. 'I believe my grandfather is organising that his estate manager will drive you to Aberdeen airport,' he added harshly.

Sabina preceded the two men down the winding staircase, anxious to be gone now. Once she was away from here perhaps she would be able to see her feelings towards Brice for what they were—be able to know if it really was love she felt towards him. Or something else.

Although none of that changed the fact that she had to end her engagement to Richard...

CHAPTER THIRTEEN

IT WAS only Brice's anger that kept him silent as he followed the couple down the stairs, the feeling of complete impotence where Sabina was concerned.

Because if he once started to speak, to protest at Sabina leaving like this, then he knew he wouldn't be able to stop, that everything he wanted to say to her about the rightness of what she was doing would come tumbling out!

How could she leave with Richard Latham after the kisses she had just shared with Brice? And she had responded, he was absolutely sure of it.

But she was still leaving with Latham...

Jeff, the estate manager, was waiting outside with the car, opening the boot so that the luggage could be stowed away.

'No matter what your feelings at the moment, Sabina,' Brice rasped as she would have moved to get into the back of the car, 'I think you should at least say goodbye to your mother. And a thank-you to my grandfather for his hospitality wouldn't go amiss, either,' he added scathingly.

A slight flush had entered her cheeks at the obvious rebuke as she straightened. 'Of course,' she acquiesced abruptly.

'It doesn't need both of you to say thank you,' Brice told Richard as he would have accompanied Sabina back into the castle.

'It's okay, Richard,' Sabina assured as the other man looked at her enquiringly. 'I'll only be a few minutes.' She squeezed his arm reassuringly, much to Brice's displeasure. He couldn't bear the thought of Sabina touching the other man even casually, let alone, let alone—

This was a living hell!

Hell wasn't what all the prophets of doom predicated it was, it wasn't fire and brimstone, an eternal purgatory. Hell was realising you were in love with a woman who was living with another man!

Because he was in love with Sabina, had known it earlier when he hadn't been able to let her leave without holding her one last time.

He didn't know how it had happened, when it had happened, he only knew that he loved everything about her, her beauty, her unaffectedness, her warmth, the huskiness of her voice, the way she moved—her loyalty to a man who didn't deserve to even kiss one of her beautiful feet!

And the thought of never seeing Sabina again gave Brice an ache in his chest that just wouldn't go away...

Hell, he now knew, was loving the unattainable!

'They'll be in my grandfather's private sitting-room,' he told Sabina harshly as she hesitated in the hallway.

She winced at the aggression in his tone. 'Brice, I—' She moistened dry lips. 'I just need a little time to—to adjust, to my mother's—friendship with your grandfather.' She looked at him pleadingly. 'It's been rather a shock,' she added emotionally.

Brice looked at her coldly, knowing that, for the moment, he daredn't look at her any other way; if he did, he wouldn't be able to stop himself from telling her how he felt about her. Which, in the circumstances, was probably the last complication she wanted to hear!

He shook his head. 'You seemed to like my grandfather well enough before you knew of his involvement with your mother,' he reminded harshly.

'I did—do like him,' she amended awkwardly.

'He just isn't your father,' Brice guessed scathingly.

Sabina's eyes flashed deeply blue. 'No, he isn't,' she conceded tersely. 'But—'

'Have you given any thought to how lonely your mother

has been the last five years?' Brice attacked impatiently. 'What it must have been like for her? From the little you've told me about your parents, I would guess that they shared a relationship of emotional and academic equality. Soul mates, in fact,' he rasped. 'I would say your mother has been living only half a life the last five years, feeling as if she's had her right arm amputated!'

Brice already felt like that over Sabina, couldn't even begin to imagine what it must be like to lose a partner after thirty or more years of marriage, to lose Sabina after spending all those years with her at his side.

'Be nice to them, Sabina,' he warned harshly.

Her brows arched derisively. 'Or else what, Brice...?' she challenged softly.

'Or else you'll have me to answer to,' he came back gratingly.

She gave a humourless smile. 'How terrifying,' she returned dismissively.

Brice only just resisted the impulse to reach out and pull her into his arms, taking a step backwards instead. 'It could be,' he assured her grimly before turning to stride forcefully down the hallway to his grandfather's sitting-room.

The older couple were standing close together across the room when Brice and Sabina entered, and if Brice wasn't mistaken there was the trace of tears on Joan's face.

'Take care,' Brice warned Sabina softly.

Her eyes flashed back a warning of her own before she turned to the other couple. 'Richard and I are leaving now.' She spoke huskily. 'I—I just wanted to say goodbye,' she added awkwardly.

Joan squeezed Hugh's arm reassuringly before turning to her daughter. 'I hope my being here hasn't chased you away?' she said gruffly.

'Of course not,' Sabina assured her lightly. 'Richard has to get back to London anyway. He has a few things to do before we fly out to Australia on Monday.'

Brice had forgotten she was going away with the other man, that the trip had been delayed because of coming up here. Obviously nothing that had happened this weekend had affected Sabina's decision to go with Richard...

Joan nodded, obviously used to her daughter's jet-setting lifestyle. 'Call me when you get back, won't you, Sabina?'

Sabina looked mildly surprised by the request, but she nodded anyway. 'Perhaps you and—and Hugh, would like to have dinner when we get back?' she suggested tentatively.

Well, at least she was trying, Brice conceded grudgingly—even if he didn't particularly care for the idea of his grandfather becoming pally with Richard Latham, as Sabina's fiancé!

'That would be lovely, Sabina,' her mother accepted warmly. 'I'm sure we would love to come. Wouldn't we, Hugh?' She turned to him for confirmation.

'Love to,' Hugh confirmed abruptly. 'I'm sorry you have to leave so soon, Sabina,' he added slightly reprovingly. 'I would have liked the chance to get to know you a little better.'

'There's no rush,' Sabina dismissed with a shrug. 'Is there?' she added less certainly.

'Depends how you look at it, I suppose,' Hugh drawled mockingly. 'After all, I'm already well past my allotted three score years and ten!'

Sabina looked at him frowningly, obviously unsure how to take this last remark. Brice knew exactly how he would have taken it—with a complete lack of seriousness. His grandfather was fit and healthy, there was absolutely no reason why he shouldn't live another ten years or more. Especially now that he had someone in his life he was obviously more than a little fond of.

Although Brice doubted, the mood she was in, that Sabina would appreciate hearing that!

'I'll call you when I get back and we'll organise dinner.' Sabina opted for safety. 'Goodbye, Brice,' she added huskily, her gaze not quite meeting his.

'I'll walk you back to the car,' he told her grimly.

She shook her head. 'There's really no need. I know the way. And—we've already said goodbye,' she added firmly.

Brice wasn't in the least happy with this arrangement, would have liked a few more minutes alone with Sabina. But he could see by the strain about her eyes, the paleness of her cheeks, that she had had enough for one day. More than enough, in fact.

He nodded abruptly. 'In that case, have a good flight back.'

'I'm sure we will.' Her smile was so fleeting it barely registered as being one, before she turned and hurried from the room.

As if she were being pursued by something particularly unpleasant, Brice acknowledged impatiently.

He turned sharply to his grandfather. 'Now, if you wouldn't mind formally introducing me to Joan…?' he prompted dryly. 'That way I'm hoping she won't find me too rude when I ask her what happened in Sabina's life a few months ago to bring about the change in her that Joan mentioned earlier!'

Because he was determined to get to the bottom of that mysterious remark. Wanted to know. Needed to know!

'All right?' Richard prompted as Sabina got into the back of the car beside him.

'Fine,' she dismissed abruptly before turning her head to have one last glance at Hugh McDonald's castle home.

It looked beautiful bathed in the May sunshine; serene, calm, a bastion of tranquillity—everything Sabina knew that she wasn't at this moment!

She had left with Richard because, in the circumstances,

she couldn't see that there was any other way. She was totally shaken by the discovery that Hugh McDonald was the man in her mother's life. But she was more shaken still by her response to Brice's kisses a few minutes ago. If Richard hadn't come into the bedroom when he had, she had no idea where it would have all ended.

Which was another reason she had to leave with Richard...

She had no idea if Richard had guessed she had been in Brice's arms only seconds before he'd entered the room, but she did know she couldn't go on with this any more, that she would have to break their engagement. That, in the circumstances, it was the only fair thing to do for Richard...

'That was a bit of a turn-up for the books, wasn't it?' he remarked lightly at her side.

Sabina turned to him blankly. 'What was?'

'Your mother and McDonald,' Richard murmured derisively. 'Still, if she had to find herself an ageing lover, at least he's a rich one!' he added scathingly.

Sabina was very conscious of Hugh McDonald's employee seated only feet away in the front of the car, knew that he must be able to hear their conversation. In fact, from the stiff way he now sat behind the steering wheel, she was sure he had.

Nevertheless, she couldn't let the remark pass by undefended. 'I'm sure Hugh's wealth has nothing to do with my mother's feelings towards him,' she said slightly indignantly.

'No?' Richard raised sceptical brows over cynical blue eyes. 'I wouldn't be too sure of that.' He shrugged uninterestedly.

Sabina would, knew that her mother had never been interested in material wealth. Goodness knew, Sabina had offered to make her mother's life a little easier financially dozens of times, only for her mother to smilingly refuse, claiming that she had enough for what she needed, which was her little cottage in Scotland, and her vast collection of books.

Besides, Hugh had so much more to recommend him than just his obvious wealth, was still handsome in a distinguished way, was highly intelligent, which her mother would appreciate, and, last of all, Hugh was extremely charming. Like his grandson!

But there was no mistaking the slight edge to Richard's tone when he talked of her mother...

She drew in a deep breath. 'Richard—'

'Not here,' he cut in tersely, looking pointedly at the driver of the car.

Now he chose to remember the other man! Not that she was averse to cancelling their talk until they were on their own; she wasn't exactly enjoying this conversation herself.

'We'll talk once we're back in London,' Richard added harshly.

Once they had returned to the home she shared with Richard. Which, she accepted heavily, would also have to change. In fact, everything would have to change once she had explained to Richard that she could no longer keep her side of their bargain.

Although she didn't think it was a good idea to tell him it was because she had realised she was in love with Brice!

Brice...

How her heart ached just at the thought of him, more and more so as the miles between them lengthened. When would she ever see Brice again? She had made her feelings concerning the portrait more than plain, as had Richard, which meant, ironically, that the only link she now had with Brice was through her mother's relationship with Hugh.

Poetic justice for her own unreasonableness the other week when her mother had tried to tell her of the new friendship in her life?

Probably, Sabina conceded heavily as she finally relaxed back in her seat. Something else she knew she would have to put right at the earliest opportunity.

But first she had to sever her engagement to Richard...

Not a pleasant thought, the brief sideways glance she gave in his direction showing her that at the moment he looked grimly unapproachable. This was going to be far from easy!

But, then, why should it be? Richard had been completely honest from the beginning about what he wanted from her in their engagement, and what he would give in return. And he had kept his side of the bargain. Richard hadn't changed; she was the one who had done that. Worse, she had fallen in love with another man. Although, she hoped she wouldn't actually have to tell Richard that part. It was enough that she could no longer continue with their engagement, without involving Brice in its demise.

Especially as Brice had no idea she had fallen in love with him!

And he never would have. It was enough of a folly that she knew she was in love with him, without Brice being embarrassed by the knowledge too. Besides, if her mother's relationship with Hugh became something more permanent, she and Brice were going to be related in some way. In which case, Brice must never know that she had been stupid enough to fall in love with him!

'The sitting-room, I think,' Richard announced grimly hours later when they finally reached the house, marching straight over to the array of drinks and pouring out a large measure of brandy.

It had not been a particularly pleasant journey back to London, Richard not inclined to conversation during the flight or the drive back into the City from the airport. In fact, Sabina felt in need of a brandy herself!

'Could I have one of those?' she prompted huskily.

Richard wordlessly poured a measure of brandy into a

second glass before handing it to her. 'Dutch courage, Sabina?' he finally rasped as he stepped back, his gaze hard as he looked at her through narrowed lids.

He did know about the kisses she had shared with Brice earlier; Sabina was sure of it now as she looked at the hard accusation in Richard's face. Well-deserved accusation, she acknowledged heavily.

'I'm going to save you the trouble of breaking our engagement, Sabina,' Richard continued harshly. 'And break it myself!' he added scathingly. 'I'm sure I made clear to you from the onset what I wanted from you, that I never deal with imperfection!'

Sabina gasped at the look of disgust that accompanied this savagely made insult. 'I've never claimed to be perfect, Richard,' she began softly.

'"Never claimed to be perfect"'! he echoed scornfully. 'You didn't need to claim it—I knew you were. Successful, beautiful, coolly self-composed, untouched,' he added the last forcefully. 'Most of all, untouched! But that's no longer true, is it?' he accused hardly.

She had known Richard was going to be upset when she broke their engagement, but nothing had prepared her for this venomous attack. She had seen Richard angry with other people in the past, but for the main part she had refused to see the callousness with which he could deal with people who had disappointed him. Well, now she had disappointed him—and nothing was going to save her from feeling the sharp edge of that rapier tongue!

She shook her head. 'I don't know what you mean—'

'I mean coming into that bedroom earlier today and finding you still all hot and sweaty from being in Brice McAllister's arms!' Richard cut in icily.

'Hot and sweaty...?' Sabina repeated incredulously. 'Richard, you're being—'

'Crudely honest?' he concluded distastefully. 'Maybe that's because that's exactly what this is.' He shook his head disgustedly. 'I thought you were different, Sabina. I thought, after what happened to you, that you were a person, like me, removed from this physical thrashing about people so often associate with love, that you wanted the things from a relationship that we've had together the last few months: companionship, intelligent conversation, mutual admiration and liking, while at the same time retaining one's personal integrity.' He gave another shake of his head. 'But this weekend—your behaviour with McAllister has shown me that you're just like every other woman!'

Sabina stared at him with complete disbelief for what she was hearing. She had shared this house with Richard for several months now, had thought that she knew him. But the things he was saying to her now told her that she clearly didn't!

'And to think,' he continued disgustedly, 'I was actually thinking of asking you to marry me!' He shook his head.

She had noted his comment about a honeymoon on the drive up to Scotland, remembered several comments Brice had made about Richard's wedding plans. But she had thought they had only been made to give credence to their engagement. She had obviously been wrong...

Sabina moistened dry lips. 'That was never part of our agreement.'

Richard gave her a scathing glance. 'Your behaviour with McAllister has put our "agreement" at an end, Sabina,' he told her coldly. 'In the circumstances, I would appreciate it if you would remove yourself, and your belongings, from my home as quickly as possible.'

Sabina stared at him. He had a right to feel angry, she accepted that, but this was a Richard she had never seen before. A man she didn't want to know, either...

CHAPTER FOURTEEN

'THIS is getting to be quite a habit.' Chloe spoke lightly as she sat beside Brice.

His scowl didn't lighten at the teasingly made remark, his attention all focused on the catwalk in front of him as he waited for the lights to go down and the fashion show to begin.

He had been trying for the last three weeks to see, or at least speak to, Sabina, only succeeding in receiving the proverbial brush-off from Richard Latham's watchdog housekeeper every time he'd telephoned the house; Sabina was either 'away', or 'unavailable'. Brice had a feeling she was only unavailable to him!

And so he had once again resorted to persuading Chloe into letting him accompany her to a fashion show where he knew Sabina was to be the top model on the catwalk.

These last three weeks Brice had felt like a thirsty man in a desert—but his thirst was for sight and sound of Sabina, not water!

'Don't get too used to it,' he told Chloe dryly. 'This really isn't my thing.'

Chloe gave him a knowing look. 'I'm not completely stupid, Brice,' she drawled.

He grinned at his cousin-in-law. 'I never for a moment thought you were!' She would have bored his cousin Fergus in the first week if that were the case, instead of which the two of them were more in love than ever.

'It was rather a surprise for all of us when Hugh announced his intention of getting remarried,' Chloe remarked innocently.

Too innocently, Brice knew. But he had probably been

153

the least surprised of them all when Hugh had telephoned each member of the family last weekend to make his announcement. Yet another reason he needed to speak to Sabina. At least, that was what he told himself...

'To Sabina's mother, of all people,' Chloe continued conversationally.

'So I believe,' he acknowledged dismissively.

He didn't 'believe' it at all—he knew it. And he desperately wanted to know how Sabina had taken the news.

Chloe arched dark brows. 'Fergus tells me you've already met Joan...?'

'Briefly,' he confirmed tersely, having no intention of filling any of his family in on that disaster of a weekend. Not that meeting Joan had been a disaster, far from it, but as for the rest of the weekend...! 'Don't worry, Chloe,' he drawled, 'you'll get your chance next weekend when we're all invited to the formal introduction to our soon-to-be stepgrandmother!'

When was this show going to start? he wondered impatiently. It was scheduled to start at eight-thirty, but it was almost nine o'clock now!

'I'm not worried, Brice,' Chloe assured him dryly. 'I know Hugh well enough to accept he has impeccable taste; I'm sure Joan is lovely. Will Sabina be there next weekend, do you think?'

If Chloe meant to divert him from his scowling contemplating of the catwalk with the suddenness of her question, then she succeeded. Whether or not Sabina intended being at the dinner at a London hotel next weekend was one of the things he had been wondering about himself!

He certainly hoped it was to be the case, and not just for selfish reasons; he had come to like Joan very much over the last few weeks, and he wouldn't like Sabina to do anything that might hurt her mother—and ultimately herself.

'I have no idea,' he dismissed blandly. 'Are these things usually as late starting as this?' he added impatiently.

'Invariably,' Chloe confirmed unconcernedly. 'Don't worry, Brice.' She reached over and squeezed his arm reassuringly. 'I have it on good authority that Sabina is definitely here.'

No doubt with the ever-watchful Clive in attendance! Well, that was just too bad—because he intended seeing Sabina this evening, no matter who might try to stop him.

'I don't—' He broke off as the lights began to dim, the loud music that seemed to accompany all these functions suddenly blasting out over the speakers. 'And about time, too!' he muttered irritably, settling himself more comfortably in his seat as he prepared to see Sabina for the first time in three weeks.

During the next hour model after model came strutting down the catwalk, all of them dramatically beautiful in the designer clothing—and none of them was Sabina!

'She *is* here, Brice,' Chloe assured him again as she sensed his tension rising by the minute.

He scowled darkly. 'Then where the he—' He broke off, half a dozen spotlights suddenly focused on the centre of the stage, the music stopping briefly as the finale of the first half of this fashion show began.

Sabina...!

Beautiful, mysterious, alluring Sabina. She looked exquisite in the sparkling dress of midnight blue, the material shimmering suggestively about the perfect curves of her body as she seemed to glide down the centre catwalk, blonde hair arranged in a fantastic space-age style, the dramatic eye make-up she wore making her eyes appear the same midnight-blue as the glittering dress she wore. She looked to neither left nor right as she came to a halt at the end of the catwalk, but her smile seemed to glow almost as much as that sensually entrancing gown.

Brice was too stunned by her appearance to join in the

enthusiastic applause of the rest of the audience. Sabina had never looked so beautiful to him.

Or so aloof and unattainable!

This was her world, he realised numbly, the world where she was Queen. And he, he suddenly realised, he was chasing that elusive 'end of the rainbow'...

He was paralysed by the realisation, didn't even register the fact that Sabina, after smiling and waving to the enthusiastic audience, had now left the catwalk, the main lights coming back on for the brief interval.

'Do you want to go behind the scenes now?' Chloe asked gently, seeming aware that Brice was totally transfixed.

Even if she had no idea of the reason for it...

'Brice...?' Chloe prompted again after a few seconds when she had received no response.

He pulled himself together with effort, shaking his head self-derisively. 'I'm just fooling myself, aren't I?' he muttered disgustedly. 'This is where Sabina belongs.' Here, and, as Brice was only too painfully aware, in Richard Latham's home.

'I'm not sure I agree with you there.' Chloe shook her head as they joined the other people going outside to stretch their legs before the resumption of the show. 'Most of the models I know, when they aren't actually working, lead a very lonely life. The majority, having reached the fame and fortune they thought they wanted, would give anything for the normality of genuine love and marriage in their lives,' she added softly.

'Sabina already has that,' Brice returned harshly, feeling slightly claustrophobic amongst this glittering, noisy crowd.

Chloe looked thoughtful. 'Do you really think so?' she mused frowningly. 'I've always thought of David's Uncle Richard as rather a cold man.'

Bruce shrugged. 'He's Sabina's choice, not mine,' he rasped.

But even if it meant meeting the other man again—something he had no wish to do!—he knew that for Joan's sake Sabina had to be at the dinner party next week.

He had briefly, while dazzled by Sabina's beauty and success, lost sight of the compelling reason for his being here tonight. Oh, he wanted to see her for himself, but he had told himself the driving force behind his appearance here this evening was to ascertain a promise from Sabina that she would be supportive of her mother next week.

He had told himself that…

But one look at Sabina and he had known he was only fooling himself; if anything, the love he had realised he felt towards her three weeks ago had intensified. To the point where he wasn't sure he could see her without telling her how he felt!

'Maybe it would be better if I just left now,' he acknowledged heavily.

'I don't think—' Chloe broke off what she had been about to say as they were joined by a third person. 'Hello, Annie,' she greeted the young girl warmly. 'It's going well, isn't it?'

'You should see the chaos out the back,' the young girl said with feeling before turning to Brice, giving him a cheeky grin. 'Would you be Mr McAllister?'

'I would,' he confirmed warily, completely baffled by the fact that this girl Annie was looking for him. For one thing, she was dressed casually in jeans and a tee shirt, which meant she certainly wasn't part of this glittering, well-dressed crowd. Also, she had mentioned 'out the back'.

'Then this is for you.'' Annie thrust an envelope into his hand. 'Back to the chaos!' She grimaced before hurrying off, pushing her way unconcernedly through the crowd.

Brice looked down dazedly at the envelope he now held. What on earth—?

'Aren't you going to open it?' Chloe prompted curiously after several minutes of Brice just staring at the envelope. 'Annie is one of the dressers from backstage,' she added helpfully.

Brice had already guessed that much. And as he only knew one person backstage, this letter had to have come from Sabina. So much for his thinking she had been completely unaware of her audience earlier. That was professionalism for you; Sabina, although giving no outward sign of it, had obviously been aware enough to see him sitting out there with Chloe!

But why would Sabina be writing to him? To warn him, having seen him and guessed his intention, not to embarrass himself by trying to see her later this evening when the show was over? Or was it something else? He was almost afraid of the answer to that!

'Just open it and see what she has to say,' Chloe encouraged impatiently as he still hesitated.

Brice gave her a mocking glance. 'Aren't you assuming rather a lot?' he drawled.

'I doubt it,' his cousin-in-law told him dismissively. 'Look, I'll be back in a few minutes. I'm going to the ladies' room for the dozenth time this evening.' She grimaced, the discomforts of early pregnancy already having made themselves felt. 'It will also give you a chance to read your letter in peace,' she urged, squeezing his arm encouragingly before hurrying off.

If Chloe weren't already married to, and deeply in love with, his own cousin, Brice knew he could have fallen in love with her himself at that moment just for her thoughtfulness alone. If, that was, he didn't already love Sabina so deeply!

'If you need to talk to me just show this letter to one

of the security men at the end of the show', Sabina's letter read.

Brice turned the single sheet of paper over just to check there was nothing else written there. There wasn't.

Very helpful! If he needed to talk to her—not that she wanted to talk to him.

Whatever that might mean!

Sabina wasn't sure, looking at the uncompromising expression on Brice's face as he stood in front of the closed door of her tiny changing-room, that this had been a good idea. In fact, the ache in her chest, just at the sight of him, told her that it wasn't.

But she had been completely thrown earlier this evening when she'd seen Brice in the audience seated next to the designer, and his cousin-by-marriage, Chloe Fox—had been sure that he couldn't possibly be here to see the show. Which had to mean he was here to see her. At least, she had thought he was. As she looked at the harshness of his expression now, she wasn't so sure...!

Not that any of that uncertainty showed in her expression as she sat down and turned back to the mirror to start removing the heavy make-up she had needed for the show, looking at his reflection enquiringly. 'What did you think of this evening?'

He grimaced, making no move to come further into the room. 'I have little experience of these things, but it looked okay to me.' He shrugged dismissively.

She couldn't help but smile at the predictability of his reply. 'How have you been, Brice?' she prompted lightly, dressed in her own clothes now, casual fitted denims and a bright red tee shirt, her hair loosely curling down the length of her spine.

'How have I—?' He broke off abruptly, taking a deep, controlling breath. 'I'm sure you didn't invite me back here to indulge in pleasantries,' he rasped.

Sabina calmly continued the ritual of removing her make-up, hoping that Brice wouldn't see the tell-tale shake of her hand just the sight of him produced. 'And I'm equally sure you didn't come here this evening to watch a fashion show,' she returned as scathingly.

'Oh? Then why am I here?' he returned unhelpfully.

Sabina shrugged. 'At a guess, I would say you wanted to see me to make certain that I will be at your grandfather's dinner party next weekend,' she drawled knowingly.

'And will you?' he challenged.

She swallowed down her disappointment as she realised she had been right about Brice's reason for being here this evening. Part of her had hoped—

She should have known better. It had all been a game to Brice, the kisses, the flirtation. A dangerous game admittedly, but a game, nonetheless.

Her eyes flashed angrily as she looked at his reflection in the mirror. 'I'm not sure I particularly like the fact that you believe I could ever hurt my mother by not being there,' she bit out tautly.

He raised dark brows. 'Does that mean you are going?'

She glared at him in the mirror. 'Not that it's any of your business—but, yes, I will be there,' she told him dismissively. 'Was that all?' she challenged, more angry than she cared to admit at his lack of faith in her.

More disappointed than she cared to admit that this was his only reason for wanting to see her.

But what had she expected? That Brice would have missed her as much as she had him the last three weeks? That he had also hungered just for the sight and sound of her? As she had hungered for him…

'No, it is not all!' Brice rasped from behind her.

Very close behind her, she acknowledged a little shakily, Brice having moved swiftly across the room, now standing so close Sabina could feel the heat emanating from his body.

He looked about them impatiently, the room in complete chaos from her hurried changes in the second half of the fashion show. 'Have you finished here now?' he asked. 'Or are you going on to the inevitable party that always seems to follow one of these things?' he added scornfully.

'Parties that I, invariably, choose not to attend,' she reminded dryly.

He nodded abruptly. 'Where's the attentive Clive this evening?' he rasped.

Truthfully, she had no idea. But she wasn't about to tell Brice that… 'Night off,' she dismissed lightly.

'Latham?' he rasped harshly.

'Still in Australia.' As far as she knew.

He gave a mocking inclination of his head. 'In that case, shall we go and have coffee together somewhere?' he suggested huskily.

She looked at him with narrowed eyes. 'What about Chloe?'

Brice shrugged. 'She already left.'

Should she have coffee with him? Her life had changed dramatically during the last three weeks, although Brice could know nothing of that. No one knew. Not even her mother. And, for the moment, Sabina wanted it to remain that way.

But there was no reason, just because she and Brice had coffee together, that he should guess just how different her life was from the last time she had seen him. No reason whatsoever.

'I know what happened to you last November, Sabina.'

The words, for all that they were softly spoken, sliced through the atmosphere like a knife, Sabina turning sharply to look up at Brice. Yes, she could see by the compassion in that emerald-green gaze that he did know.

The last thing she wanted from Brice was his pity—now, or ever!

'So what?' She shrugged dismissively. 'My mother told you, I suppose?' she added disgustedly.

'Only because I asked her,' Brice defended.

'And that makes it okay, does it?' Sabina stood up abruptly, moving sharply away from him, shaking her head disgustedly as she did so.

He shrugged. 'Your mother is a very honest and straightforward woman.'

'And I'm not?' She raised challenging brows.

'I didn't say that—'

'What happened isn't something I ever wanted to become public knowledge,' she snapped impatiently. In fact she had gone to great pains to ensure that it didn't.

'And I'm not the public!' Brice came back harshly. 'In a few weeks' time we'll all be part of the same family!'

Sabina faced him tensely. 'My mother marrying your grandfather does not make us "family",' she scorned dismissively.

His mouth tightened ominously. 'It does in my book.'

'That's your prerogative,' she returned heatedly.

She didn't want to be related to this man. She loved him, ached to be with him all the time. The thought of them occasionally meeting at 'family' get-togethers sounded painful in the extreme. Especially as one day Brice was sure to arrive at one of those get-togethers with the woman he intended marrying!

'Damn it, Sabina, I didn't come here this evening to get into an argument with you in this hell-hole!' Brice rasped, obviously at the end of his own patience too.

This 'hell-hole' was pure luxury compared to some of the conditions the other models had worked in this evening. Although she knew what Brice meant; it was an airless, windowless room, of very small proportions.

She gave the ghost of a smile. 'Where did you intend getting into an argument with me, then?' she returned mockingly. It was what they inevitably seemed to do whenever they met!

Brice didn't return her smile, a nerve pulsing in the rigid line of his jaw. 'Are you going to have coffee with me or not?' he pushed forcefully.

'I—' She broke off her angry refusal. If she said no, the next time she saw Brice would be at the first of those family get-togethers next weekend. 'I am,' she stated firmly instead, having applied a lip gloss as her only make-up now, picking up her jacket in preparation for leaving.

Brice gave an impatient sigh. 'Why couldn't you have just said that in the first place?' He reached out to take a light hold of her arm, as if he expected her to take flight in the other direction as soon as they were out of the room.

Sabina gave him a mocking smile. 'I couldn't make it that easy for you, Brice,' she taunted.

He gave a disgusted shake of his head. 'Believe me, I've never found anything about being around you *easy*, Sabina,' he bit out grimly.

She gave him a searching look, wondering exactly what he meant by that remark. Or maybe she was just looking for something that wasn't there. Wishful thinking.

'Come on, then, Brice.' She walked out into the hallway as he held the door open for her. 'I have my car outside.'

He raised dark brows as they strolled towards the exit. 'That's new, isn't it?'

'Not at all, I've been driving for years,' she told him off-handedly.

'That isn't exactly what I mean,' Brice rasped impatiently.

Sabina had known exactly what he'd meant, knew he was referring to the fact that she was now driving herself again rather than being driven around by other people.

It was the least of the changes that had taken place in her life in the last three weeks…

CHAPTER FIFTEEN

'THERE'S something different about you tonight,' Brice murmured slowly as the two of them sat in the lounge of a leading London hotel, the tray of coffee they had ordered having already been placed on the table in front of Sabina.

Was that a wariness in her gaze as she looked up at him? Or was he imagining it? The look was so fleeting, before it was masked by a polite smile, that he really couldn't be sure...

'Is there?' Sabina dismissed lightly, handing him the cup of black coffee he had asked for before sitting back in her chair to sip her own coffee. 'I'm always a little hyper after a show, so perhaps that's it?' She shrugged.

'Nice car,' he commented lightly on the sporty powder-blue Mercedes she had driven here.

'Thanks,' she dismissed. 'I'm actually enjoying driving in London again,' she added happily.

She had changed, Brice mused frowningly as he registered that smile. That fear he had sensed in her from the first time he had seen her no longer seemed to be there. Although, of course, he now knew the reason it had been there in the first place...

'Your mother really wasn't breaking a confidence by talking to me, you know, Sabina,' he sat forward to tell her huskily. 'She believed—perhaps erroneously—that the two of us are friends,' he added with a self-derisive grimace.

A shutter came down over the previous candidness of Sabina's gaze. 'I'm not the first public figure—and I'm sure I won't be the last, either!—to receive threatening

164

letters and phone calls from someone who doesn't like what I do.' She shrugged dismissively.

Bruce wasn't so easily put off, knew from Joan that there had been more to it than that. 'The man actually broke into your dressing-room at a show one evening and attacked you,' he said huskily, feeling murderous himself at the thought of anyone trying to harm Sabina.

As he had when Joan had first told him what had happened to Sabina to put that fear into her eyes, to turn her into someone almost afraid of her own shadow, into someone that Joan barely recognised any more.

Brice had burned with anger after talking to Joan, had wanted to get hold of the man who had attacked her and— Most of all he had wanted to pick Sabina up, wrap her in the cloak of his protection, and make sure that nothing like that ever happened to her again.

Except Richard Latham had already done that...

He had also been filled with a need to hit the other man because he was the one being allowed to protect Sabina!

Sabina shrugged, still avoiding the directness of Brice's gaze. 'He agreed to be put under psychiatric care for his actions that night,' she stated flatly. 'Which is why it was never taken any further.'

It was also the reason that the incident had never become public knowledge. Oh, Brice could see why Sabina preferred it to be that way. He just couldn't rid himself of the mental image of a female celebrity who had been shot dead in similar circumstances a couple of years ago.

'Look, Brice.' Sabina sat forward agitatedly. 'That's all over now, and—'

'Is it?' he rasped harshly. 'What about the letters you're still receiving?'

He was taking a risk on guessing she was still receiving those threatening letters, but one look at her stricken face and he knew that he had guessed correctly about that distinctive green envelope, the one that had arrived in the post and that she had reacted to so strangely that day he'd called to see her.

His mouth twisted angrily. 'I don't think the *psychiatric care* has been too successful—do you?'

The slenderness of her throat moved convulsively as she swallowed hard. She drew in a harsh breath. 'Brice, I really would rather not discuss this.' She shook her head agitatedly.

'I can understand that,' he acknowledged heavily. 'But the man hasn't stopped, has he? He's obviously just biding his time until he has the chance to get to you again. He—'

'Stop!' Sabina cut in harshly. 'Just stop this, Brice,' she said shakily. 'I— The letters have stopped. I haven't received one for weeks now.' She shook her head.

'At a guess I would say you had received another one the day I called to see you and you were "ill" in bed,' he guessed shrewdly.

Sabina's gaze flickered briefly across his face before being averted once again. 'You're very astute, Brice,' she told him huskily. 'I— That was the last one I received.'

'Four weeks ago.' He nodded. 'How often were you receiving them before that?' His gaze was narrowed questioningly.

She swallowed again. 'Every couple of weeks,' she acknowledged huskily,

'A little early to presume there will be no more, don't you think?' Brice rasped, the anger he felt towards this unknown man making him sound harsh.

Sabina opened her mouth to say something, and then obviously thought better of it, shrugging instead.

'Sabina…?' Brice looked at her questioningly. 'What is it you aren't telling me?' he prompted slowly, more convinced by the moment that there was something.

She forced a bright smile to her lips. 'Goodness, there must be lots of things I'm not telling you, Brice,' she dismissed lightly. 'We don't know each other well enough to share confidences!'

Didn't know—! Brice drew in a sharp breath. He *knew* this woman well enough to know he was in love with her, that he thought of nothing else but her, night and day—how much better did he need to know her?

'Thanks!' he snapped irritatedly.

'You're welcome.' She gave him that mischievous grin again.

Brice gave her a reproving frown. 'You've obviously been very busy the last three weeks.' So busy that she had either been 'out' or 'unavailable' every time he'd telephoned her!

Again he sensed that sudden wariness in her. Not that old fear that he now knew the reason for, just wariness. Why?

'I did tell you weeks ago that my schedule is very heavily booked for the next six months,' she returned noncommittally.

'So you did,' he drawled. 'I haven't been exactly idle the last three weeks myself,' he added dryly.

'Oh?' She gave him a look of polite interest.

A look Brice instantly resented. The last thing he wanted from Sabina was her politeness!

'I've finished the portrait,' he told her abruptly.

She blinked. 'My portrait?'

He gave a mocking inclination of his head. 'None other,' he drawled.

A flush darkened her cheeks. 'But—I—I didn't finish sitting for it,' she said agitatedly. 'Besides, I—you—Richard told you he no longer wanted it,' she concluded awkwardly.

Brice's eyes narrowed angrily. 'Do you think so little of my artistic talent that you believe I'm incapable of painting a subject without having them sit in front of me for hours at a time?' he rasped.

'No! But—' She made a dismissive movement. 'Why bother when you no longer have a—a client, to sell it to?' She gave a perplexed frown. 'I suppose that I could always—'

'It isn't for sale!' Brice cut in harshly.

He had sat and finished Sabina's portrait for his own sake, for the sake of his sanity, it had felt like at times. Painting her image on canvas had been his only way of feeling in the least close to her this last three weeks!

And, even if he did say so himself, it was a wonderful portrait; Sabina painted against the background of that room at his grandfather's castle, a wistfully beautiful Sabina, surrounded by the mystery that was such a part of her.

There was no way that Brice would ever sell it. To anyone. In the circumstances, it was just as well that Latham had changed his mind about wanting it—Brice would have had a difficult time telling the other man that the portrait was not for sale!

Sabina shook her head. 'I don't understand.'

Brice's mouth twisted sardonically. 'Don't you?'

'No.' She looked more puzzled than ever. 'What are you going to do with it?'

'I'm not sure...' he answered slowly. 'I may exhibit it.' Although the thought of letting Sabina's portrait out of his possession for a moment, even to a reputable gallery, told him that he probably wouldn't do that, either. Perhaps he would just hang it in his bedroom—it was the closest he was ever going to get to having Sabina there!

'Let me know if you decide to do that.' Sabina nodded. 'I would love to come along and see it.'

'You can come to my home at any time and do that,' Brice returned harshly.

Sabina gave a tight smile, shaking her head. 'I think I'll wait for the exhibition.'

He shrugged. 'Please yourself,' he bit out tautly.

The atmosphere between them had changed over the last few minutes, Brice realised frowningly, Sabina having lost most of that effervescence he had noticed in her earlier. And he wanted it back!

'Sabina—' He broke off abruptly, becoming very still as he watched her lift her coffee-cup to her lips, totally stunned as he realised there was something else that was different about Sabina this evening. Something he should have noticed earlier, but hadn't.

Her left hand was bare of the huge diamond ring that, to Brice, had clearly represented Richard Latham's possession of her!

Sabina looked at Brice enquiringly, realising as she did so that he was staring transfixed at her left hand. Her bare left hand.

There were several excuses she could have given him for her engagement ring not being there: she never wore it when she was modelling and had forgotten to put it back on after the show; it was at the jeweller's being made smaller—she had lost half a stone in weight the last three weeks, much to the chagrin of the people she worked with, who had had to alter the clothes she modelled—or she could just say she had forgotten to put it on this evening. But none of those excuses would have been the truth...

'Where's your ring?' Brice finally seemed to collect himself enough to ask.

Sabina made a show of looking down at her bare hands. What was Brice going to think if she told him she didn't have the ring because she was no longer engaged? The truth, probably, you idiot, she instantly remonstrated with herself—that she and Richard were no longer together! And that Brice was the reason for that...?

She sat up straighter in her armchair, her gaze very direct as she looked across at Brice. 'I have no idea what

Richard has done with it since I gave it back to him,' she told Brice evenly.

He gave a pained frown. 'You gave Latham back his engagement ring?'

'Yes,' she confirmed shortly. 'I didn't think it was right to keep it as we're no longer engaged,' she added dryly.

'When did you give it back to him?' Brice prompted slowly, very tense now.

If she said, Three weeks ago, the time she and Richard had returned from Scotland, then Brice was going to assume that he had something to do with the engagement being broken—either that Richard had guessed they had been in each other's arms that day, or—worse—that Sabina had broken the engagement because of her realised feelings for Brice. That last reason might be the correct one, but she didn't have to be stripped of all her pride!

Brice leant forward in his chair. 'I've been calling the house the last three weeks to speak to you,' he told her harshly. 'The housekeeper told me you were unavailable!'

Sabina gave a rueful smile. 'I suppose that's technically correct—I haven't lived at the house for several weeks. Look, Brice, it's very late,' she added firmly, bending to pick up her bag, 'and it's been a long evening, so if you'll excuse me—'

'No, I won't excuse you!' he burst in forcefully, his expression grim. 'You can't just get up and leave after telling me you've broken your engagement to Latham!'

'Of course I can,' she told him reasonably. 'Anyway, the engagement was broken by mutual agreement,' she added hardly. 'It's no big deal, Brice,' she dismissed lightly as Brice still scowled. 'In fact, I've quite enjoyed these last few weeks of freedom,' she added with some surprise.

Something had changed inside her the night her engagement to Richard had ended, a reassertion of her old confident self, her independence, the fear she had lived under for these last months also coming to an end that night. For a very good reason…

Her mouth tightened. 'I like being my own person again, Brice,' she told him dismissively. 'I've moved into my own apartment,' she explained. 'I do what I want, and go where I want.' She shrugged. 'I must admit I had forgotten how good that feels,' she concluded softly.

And she had. After the attack she had lived in dread of something like that happening again, had been only too glad of Richard's offer of protection. She just hadn't realised the price he'd expected her to pay for that protection…

But these last three weeks of standing on her own feet she had regained the confidence she had lost after the attack, had been determined that she had to do that. And she had succeeded. Much better than she had anticipated.

Her apartment had been chosen and paid for, furniture moved in, she had even resumed some of her social life with some of the other models, had decided that she simply couldn't live in fear of the attack being repeated, that she wanted to live the full life she had known before.

She was even—although she doubted Brice would believe it—looking forward to attending her mother's engagement dinner next weekend, was truly pleased for her mother and Hugh.

She had telephoned her mother and arranged to have lunch with her a week ago, and the two of them had talked together in a way that they never had before, had attained a closeness that Sabina cherished. And her mother, Sabina knew, would never repeat any of *that* particular conversation to Brice…!

'I see,' Brice answered her slowly. 'Then there's no point in my asking you to have dinner with me tomorrow evening?' he added harshly.

Sabina was about to facetiously agree with him that

there wasn't, and then she wavered as she saw the intensity of his expression as he waited for her answer.

She drew her breath in softly, the tension between them now so heavy she felt as if she could reach out and touch it. 'Why would you want to do that?' she delayed huskily.

'Because it's too soon to ask you to spend the rest of your life with me!' he bit out self-derisively.

Sabina's eyes widened with shock as she stared at him disbelievingly. Had Brice just said—? Had he really just—?

She shook her head dazedly, couldn't speak, daredn't speak. Was Brice telling her that he loved her?

'I take it that's a no to spending the rest of your life with me,' Brice rasped hardly as he obviously saw that shake of her head. 'Okay, then I'll settle for the dinner together I originally asked for!'

He was going too fast for her—she was still trying to get over the shock of his last statement! How had he jumped from dinner to a lifetime together? Had she missed something?

'Could we just go back a few steps, Brice?' she said slowly, looking at him uncertainly now. 'I know you've flirted with me the last couple of months, that you've even kissed me—'

'Let me just put you straight about something before you continue, Sabina,' he cut in firmly. 'I don't flirt. I never have. I never will,' he stated flatly.

'But—'

'As for the kisses,' he continued as if uninterrupted. 'It was a question of kissing you or putting you over my knee and spanking you—I chose the more pleasurable option. For myself!'

Sabina swallowed hard, a bubble of happiness starting to build up inside her as she listened to him. A fragile bubble she was very much afraid would suddenly be burst!

'Brice, could we get out of here?' She frowned. 'Go

somewhere where we can talk less publicly?' The lounge of this busy hotel was still full of people, despite it being after midnight.

He looked at her for several long minutes before answering. 'Can I have your agreement to have dinner with me tomorrow first?' he finally said slowly.

If what she thought—hoped—was true, he could have her promise for more than that!

But she didn't say that, just nodded, still too stunned to dare to believe what Brice was saying to her.

'Good enough,' Brice bit out forcefully, standing up. 'Okay, let's go.'

Sabina shyly took the hand he held out to her as she got slowly to her feet, leaving her hand nestling within the warm confines of his as they walked out into the night.

CHAPTER SIXTEEN

BRICE had never felt so nervous in his entire life as he poured Sabina and himself a glass of brandy. Admittedly Sabina had left the hotel with him, driven them both back to his home, but he was still uncertain of her motive for doing so. Did she just want to let him down gently, away from that crowded hotel? Or was it something else?

'There we are.' He crossed the sitting-room to where Sabina sat in one of the armchairs, handing her the glass of brandy before taking a sip of his own. Although the fiery liquid did little to warm him; he felt like a prisoner awaiting sentence!

'Sabina—'

'Brice—'

They both spoke together, smiling ruefully at each other as they both stopped at the same time too.

'You first,' Brice invited, remaining standing, feeling too restless to sit down. Sabina might no longer be engaged to Latham, but that didn't mean he stood a chance with her himself. In fact, the comments she had made earlier about enjoying her freedom seemed to imply the opposite. Although she had at least agreed to have dinner with him tomorrow...

Sabina drew in a deep breath before speaking, her brandy remaining untouched in the glass. 'There are some things I have to tell you before—before—'

Before 'passing the sentence'? Brice wasn't sure, after all the weeks of tension, that he could get through this. Before he had been tied by the fact that Sabina was engaged to another man, that loyalty alone—he didn't even want to think about Sabina being in love with Richard

Latham—meaning she couldn't, wouldn't respond to
Brice's interest in her. But now that excuse was out of the
way, there was still no reason to believe Sabina might be
interested in him!

'Then tell me,' he rasped more harshly than he meant
to, wincing as he saw the way she tensed at his tone. 'I'm
sorry,' he sighed. 'I'm afraid I'm not the most patient of
men,' he acknowledged ruefully.

'I would never have guessed!' She gave a slight smile.
'Anyway,' she began again, 'as I've already explained, I
am no longer engaged to Richard.' She looked straight at
Brice now, blue gaze unblinking. 'The engagement was
broken exactly three weeks ago. The moment we returned
from Scotland, in fact,' she admitted ruefully.

'Go on,' Brice encouraged huskily, almost afraid to
breathe now in case he broke the moment.

She sighed, taking a sip of the brandy before continuing.
'I was the one to broach the subject, but—Richard had
reached the same conclusion. I—' She gave a pained
frown. 'I saw a Richard that day I hadn't known existed.
A man who will go to any lengths—any lengths,' she repeated with a shudder, 'to add what he considers unique
to his already vast collection.' She looked up at Brice now,
her eyes glittering brightly with unshed tears. 'You said
earlier that it was too soon to know whether or not those
horrible letters had stopped. I can assure you that they
have,' she said gruffly. 'Because Richard was the one
sending them!'

Brice stared at Sabina, unable to take in exactly what
she was saying. How could Latham have been responsible
for sending those letters? For one thing, there had definitely been a man last November sending her letters and
making threatening telephone calls, because he had been
put under psychiatric care after his attack on Sabina.
Secondly, Latham was supposed to be in love with Sabina,

and he must have known how much receiving those letters upset her...

Or was that the point? Brice wondered sharply. Hadn't Latham's own nephew warned Brice about ever tangling with him, that his uncle was a fierce collector of priceless objects? And Sabina, although certainly not an object, was certainly priceless!

Sabina gave a humourless smile as she saw the obvious bewilderment on Brice's face. 'Hard to believe, isn't it?' she said shakily. 'I still find it difficult to believe I could ever have trusted such a man!' She shook her head self-disgustedly. 'But it is true, Brice. Richard and I argued that day when we returned from Scotland. Richard said some things that were—' She swallowed hard. 'He was angry because he guessed— He was angry,' she repeated flatly. 'And in the course of that anger he told me that once I had agreed to marry him he had been the one to take up sending me those letters.'

'But why?' Brice rasped.

Sabina grimaced. 'Can't you guess?'

'To keep you dependent on his protection!' Brice suddenly guessed furiously. 'You would obviously have been very vulnerable after that attack,' he continued frowningly. 'Very susceptible to Latham's apparent kindness, I suspect—'

'Very,' Sabina confirmed heavily. 'The truth is, Brice, Richard and I were never in love with each other. We— we made a bargain,' she admitted huskily. 'Richard would protect me, and I—I—'

'You became the priceless object on his arm,' Brice finished incredulously.

'Yes,' she admitted with a grimace. 'I *was* frightened after the attack, Brice. Completely vulnerable.' She looked at him imploringly.

'And he wanted to keep you that way,' Brice ground out angrily as he saw the whole truth now.

The bastard! How could he? How dared he do that to Sabina…?

'Exactly,' Sabina confirmed heavily. 'You mentioned that I had probably received one of those letters that day you came to the house and I was ill? That was because— Richard had come home early from a business trip that evening I came to your house and ended up staying for dinner. He—he knew where I had been.'

'Clive!' Brice guessed disgustedly.

'Yes,' Sabina sighed. 'The letter I received was my punishment for seeing you without Richard's permission. I've had several weeks to think about this, Brice, and I realise now that I received one of those letters every time Richard thought I needed reminding that I belonged to him! In fact, that was what those letters always said, just ''You're mine''.' She swallowed hard.

'I'll kill him!' Brice's fists were clenched at his sides. 'Take great delight in tearing him limb from limb!'

Sabina shook her head. 'It doesn't matter, Brice.'

'Doesn't—! It matters to me, damn it,' he ground out furiously. 'I would like to—'

'It really doesn't matter any more, Brice,' Sabina told him huskily as she stood up. 'I became engaged to Richard for reasons that were just as wrong as his own,' she admitted gruffly. 'I felt exposed, vulnerable, after the attack, and, although I had known Richard for several months before that, it wasn't until after that I actually agreed to marry him.' She shook her head. 'For the totally wrong reason, I now realise. As for Richard, he wanted to own something he thought was unique—'

'You are unique!' Brice cut in harshly.

'Maybe,' she accepted heavily. 'But although I liked Richard, I was never in love with him. Not the way I love you,' she added so softly Brice wasn't sure he had heard her correctly.

In fact, he was sure he couldn't have heard her correctly!

*　　*　　*

Sabina looked across at Brice, sympathising with his stunned expression. As stunned as hers must have been earlier when he'd told her he was asking her out to dinner because he thought it was too soon to ask her to spend the rest of her life with him!

But she had come a long way in the last three weeks, knew that the knock to her self-confidence that she had known the night she'd been attacked would have healed in the naturalness of time—without the constant reminder of those letters that had started to arrive again only weeks later! As it had healed now...

It was still difficult for her to believe that Richard had become the perpetrator of those letters. Not that it had been too difficult for him to have done so; she had confided in him totally once they'd become engaged, even down to the fact that she'd always recognised the letters because they'd arrived in a green envelope. After that, it had been easy for Richard to simply take over sending the letters whenever he'd felt inclined to reinforce her dependence on him.

She moistened dry lips. 'Richard is—a strange man, in many ways,' she began softly, not quite meeting Brice's gaze. 'Do you have any idea what it was that made him decide I was no longer perfect, after all?'

Brice still scowled. 'Does it have anything to do with me?'

Sabina gave a rueful laugh. 'Everything to do with you! Richard, it turns out, is a man who likes to admire his possessions by simply looking at them. I—he—' She paused, her cheeks becoming red. 'Richard is absolutely horrified at the thought of physical intimacy with a per-son—any person!' she emphasised frowningly.

Brice looked more stunned than ever. 'But I thought—'

'I know what you thought, Brice.' Sabina sighed. 'By mutual agreement I had my own bedroom in Richard's house, my own room if we happened to stay at a hotel.' She shook her head. 'Which was why it was no hardship for us to have separate rooms at your grandfather's home,' she added ruefully. 'That was part of our bargain too. I believed it was out of respect for our friendship, but—it appears that Richard simply finds the whole idea of physical intimacy distasteful, a breach of a person's personal integrity.' A realisation that had stunned Sabina three weeks ago.

She had become engaged to a man who not only found a physical relationship between a man and a woman repugnant, but who stooped to sending her anonymous letters in order to maintain her dependence on him.

She still couldn't believe the lucky escape she had made!

Brice shook his head. 'The man is weirder than I thought he was,' he dismissed disgustedly. 'Although that still doesn't change the fact that I intend going to see him, want to make sure he knows he is never to come near you again,' he added grimly.

Sabina shook her head unconcernedly. 'He won't,' she said with certainty. 'Richard and I have come to an understanding—another one!' she added self-derisively. 'He will stay out of my life, and that of my family and friends, and I won't tell the police that he was the one sending me anonymous letters.' Her expression was bleak. 'I think that sounds fair.'

'Not to me,' Brice rasped. 'Never seeing you again isn't nearly punishment enough for what he did to you.'

She gave a rueful grimace. 'Richard doesn't want to see me again,' she assured him. 'He no longer considers me unique, you see,' she added softly.

Brice's eyes were narrowed. 'Why doesn't he?' he said slowly.

'Several reasons.' She shrugged. 'But the main one is

that he is aware of the—physical attraction, between the two of us.'

'That's because I find it hard to be in the same room with you for six minutes without wanting to make love to you, let alone six months!' he admitted impatiently.

She laughed softly; it was exactly the same way she felt about him! 'We've been here at least fifteen minutes now,' she pointed out provocatively, her gaze alight with the love she felt towards this man.

Brice looked at her sharply, slowly relaxing as he saw the mischievous expression on her face. 'Very remiss of me,' he murmured huskily even as he crossed the room to stand in front of her. 'I love you, Sabina,' he told her forcefully. 'I want to marry you.'

'Before I answer that, I need to assure you of a few things,' she said slowly.

'Yes?' he prompted impatiently.

Sabina smiled at that show of impatience. 'I want to assure you that none of my actions—and I mean *none* of them—are now made because of any lingering fear over what happened all those months ago. It was upsetting at the time, but I'm over it now. I would have been months ago, if not for Richard's behaviour,' she added hardly. 'Do you understand what I'm saying, Brice?'

'None of your actions now are made because of any lingering fear because of what happened all those months ago,' he repeated with obvious impatience.

'Right.' She nodded her satisfaction. 'Then my answer to your previous statement is yes,' she breathed ecstatically as she moved confidently into his arms, her head nestling against the warm strength of his shoulder.

Brice looked down at her quizzically. 'Yes, I love you? Or yes, I want to marry you?'

'Yes—I love you. And yes—I'll marry you,' she answered without hesitation, that love glowing in her eyes as she looked up at him unblinkingly.

He groaned, briefly closing his eyes. 'I'm not sure I can believe this,' he admitted huskily.

She smiled at him—she could hardly believe it herself! But it was true, she and Brice loved each other, were going to marry each other. 'I'm sure we can find a way to convince you,' she murmured throatily.

He raised teasing brows. 'Are you making an improper suggestion, Miss Smith?' He feigned shock.

'I am, Mr McAllister,' she confirmed without hesitation.

Brice's arms closed possessively about her as he swept her up, his mouth forcefully claiming hers.

But Sabina didn't doubt that it was with love, caring, desire, all the things there should be between two people who loved each other and wanted to be together for the rest of their lives…

CHAPTER SEVENTEEN

'I HAVE to say, Logan, that I think Aunt Meg is taking all of this rather well,' Brice drawled in amusement before taking a sip from his champagne glass.

The two men turned to look at Logan's mother, the actress Margaret Fraser, as she stood across the room talking to Logan's wife, Darcy, the two of them cooing over the baby boy Darcy cradled so lovingly in her arms.

Brice nodded. 'I thought it was bad enough when you and Darcy made Aunt Meg a grandmother, but now she has a stepmother who's only ten years older than she is!' He turned to look across the room to where their grandfather, newly married, was standing beside his bride greeting their guests as they arrived at the wedding reception.

Joan looked absolutely lovely in her cream satin suit, but it was to the beautiful young woman who stood at her other side, Joan's maid of honour, that Brice's gaze strayed instinctively. And stopped.

Sabina.

His own wife.

Of two weeks, four days, and—he glanced at his wristwatch—three hours.

And they had been the happiest two weeks, four days and three hours, that Brice had ever known.

The dazzling smile Sabina gave him as she caught and held his gaze told him she had read his thoughts—and that she felt exactly the same way about him!

There were no longer any shadows in Sabina's eyes, only the love and happiness that was the centre of their lives together. Brice intended seeing that it remained that way.

Although it wasn't something he ever intended discussing with Sabina—for obvious reasons—he had dealt with Richard Latham in his own way, the older man left in no doubt, after their brief meeting six weeks ago, of just how rapid—and official—Brice's reaction would be if he ever threatened or came near Sabina again.

'And what are you two talking about so cosily?' Fergus drawled as he strolled over to join them, a glass of champagne in his own hand.

Logan grinned. 'How different our lives all are from eighteen months ago,' he murmured ruefully. 'For the better, I might add,' he said firmly.

Fergus gave a leisurely glance around the room, nodding his own satisfaction. 'Logan's mother, Aunt Meg, married to Darcy's father, Daniel. Logan and Darcy married with an endearing son of their own. Chloe and I married for almost a year now, and our own baby due in three months. Even Grandfather surprising us all by finding happiness with Sabina's mother. And as for this sly devil…!' He slapped Brice on the back with cousinly affection. 'I'm still not sure how you talked that beautiful woman into marrying you!' He shook his head with mock incredulity after glancing at Sabina in her sky-blue dress.

'Charm and good looks,' Brice returned mockingly.

'Oh, yes?' Logan gave him a sceptical glance.

Brice grinned. 'I've been assured it runs in the family!'

'By whom?' Fergus taunted.

'Grandfather,' Brice answered with satisfaction.

'Oh, well,' Logan drawled, 'if Grandfather said so…!' He glanced over to where their grandfather was smiling down at his new wife, his expression softening with the affection they all felt for the patriarch of their rapidly growing family. 'It's good to see him so happy again, isn't it…?'

'Very.'

'Yes.'

Fergus and Brice both answered at the same time, the three men smiling at each other with family satisfaction.

'Well, you three are all looking very pleased with yourselves.' Chloe, Fergus's wife, looked at them enquiringly as she moved to stand beside her husband.

'Very,' Darcy added questioningly as she joined them, releasing the baby into Logan's arms as he struggled to go to his father.

'And why shouldn't they?' Sabina murmured huskily as she linked her arms with Chloe's and Darcy's. 'They're married to the three of us!' she added with a mischievous grin that encompassed all of them.

Brice glowed with love and pride as he looked at her, that love becoming almost overwhelming as his gaze included all his family.

The McDonald clan was complete!

Modern Romance™
...seduction and
passion guaranteed

Tender Romance™
...love affairs that
last a lifetime

Sensual Romance™
...sassy, sexy and
seductive

Blaze™
...sultry days and
steamy nights

Medical Romance™
...medical drama on
the pulse

Historical Romance™
...rich, vivid and
passionate

27 new titles every month.

*With all kinds of Romance for
every kind of mood...*

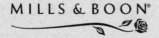

MILLS & BOON®

MB1

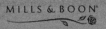

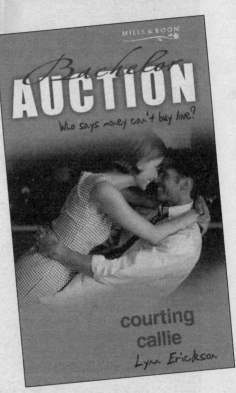

FREE

2 BOOKS
AND A SURPRISE GIFT!

We would like to take this opportunity to thank you for reading this Mills & Boon® book by offering you the chance to take TWO more specially selected titles from the Modern Romance™ series absolutely FREE! We're also making this offer to introduce you to the benefits of the Reader Service™ —

★ FREE home delivery   ★ FREE gifts and competitions
★ FREE monthly Newsletter   ★ Exclusive Reader Service discount
★ Books available before they're in the shops

Accepting these FREE books and gift places you under no obligation to buy; you may cancel at any time, even after receiving your free shipment. Simply complete your details below and return the entire page to the address below. *You don't even need a stamp!*

YES! Please send me 2 free Modern Romance™ books and a surprise gift. I understand that unless you hear from me, I will receive 4 superb new titles every month for just £2.55 each, postage and packing free. I am under no obligation to purchase any books and may cancel my subscription at any time. The free books and gift will be mine to keep in any case.

P2ZEC

Ms/Mrs/Miss/Mr ....Initials ....
BLOCK CAPITALS PLEASE
Surname ....
Address ....
....
....Postcode ....

Send this whole page to:
UK: FREEPOST CN81, Croydon, CR9 3WZ
EIRE: PO Box 4546, Kilcock, County Kildare (stamp required)

Offer valid in UK and Eire only and not available to current Reader Service subscribers to this series. We reserve the right to refuse an application and applicants must be aged 18 years or over. Only one application per household. Terms and prices subject to change without notice. Offer expires 31st December 2002. As a result of this application, you may receive offers from other carefully selected companies. If you would prefer not to share in this opportunity please write to The Data Manager at the address above.

Mills & Boon® is a registered trademark owned by Harlequin Mills & Boon Limited.
Modern Romance™ is being used as a trademark.